'Let me go, Bl

The moment he held her she wanted to turn her face up to be kissed and she knew it was a sort of madness.

'You're scared,' he murmured.

'Of course I'm not! Now, will you please stop amusing yourself at my expense?'

'I'm not amused, honey,' he said softly. He drew her close, his mouth finding hers and hardening in masculine triumph when she made no move to avoid his kiss . . .

Dear Reader

The nights are drawing in again . . . the perfect excuse for snuggling up with a Mills & Boon romance! November is the time for bonfires and fireworks, of course—and you'll find plenty of sparks flying between the heroes and heroines in this month's collection of love stories! Look out for books by some of your favourite authors . . . and, if you're missing the summer sun, why not let us transport you to sunny California and exotic Mexico? So shut out the winter darkness, and enter the warm and wonderful world of Mills & Boon!

The Editor

Patricia Wilson was born in Yorkshire and lived there until she married and had four children. She loves travelling and has lived in Singapore, Africa and Spain. She had always wanted to be a writer but a growing family and career as a teacher left her with little time to pursue her interest. With the encouragement of her family she gave up teaching in order to concentrate on writing and her other interests of music and painting.

Recent titles by the same author:

POWERFUL STRANGER
EDGE OF DANGER
SENSE OF DESTINY

RELENTLESS FLAME

BY
PATRICIA WILSON

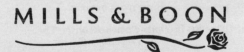

MILLS & BOON LIMITED
ETON HOUSE, 18-24 PARADISE ROAD
RICHMOND, SURREY TW9 1SR

DID YOU PURCHASE THIS BOOK WITHOUT A COVER?

If you did, you should be aware it is **stolen property** as it was reported *unsold and destroyed* by a retailer. Neither the Author nor the publisher has received any payment for this book.

All the characters in this book have no existence outside the imagination of the Author, and have no relation whatsoever to anyone bearing the same name or names. They are not even distantly inspired by any individual known or unknown to the Author, and all the incidents are pure invention.

All Rights Reserved. The text of this publication or any part thereof may not be reproduced or transmitted in any form or by any means, electronic or mechanical, including photocopying, recording, storage in an information retrieval system, or otherwise, without the written permission of the publisher.

This book is sold subject to the condition that it shall not, by way of trade or otherwise, be lent, resold, hired out or otherwise circulated without the prior consent of the publisher in any form of binding or cover other than that in which it is published and without a similar condition including this condition being imposed on the subsequent purchaser.

MILLS & BOON and the Rose Device are trademarks of the publisher.

First published in Great Britain 1994 by Mills & Boon Limited

© Patricia Wilson 1994

Australian copyright 1994   Philippine copyright 1994 This edition 1994

ISBN 0 263 78738 9

Set in Times Roman 10 on 11¼ pt. 01-9411-57851 C

Made and printed in Great Britain

CHAPTER ONE

NICOLA forced her eyes open, making herself sit up in bed. She had not really been asleep at all. She had merely been lying drowsily, waiting for the hospital to come to life around her, but even in her semi-awake state the nightmare had started, the flames had curled around her and she could still feel the scorching heat, still see the swirling, black smoke. Her heart was hammering and perspiration stood on her brow as if it was still real, still the horror she had faced.

The night sister came in and glanced at her keenly.

'Another nightmare?'

'It tried.' Nicola managed a smile, but the sister looked concerned and came to stand by the bed.

'With some people, this sort of thing goes on for a long time. It's trauma. You may need counselling when you leave here. There wasn't just the fire, after all. It was everything else.' She looked a little embarrassed, as if she had said too much, and she left rather quickly, murmuring that she had to get ready for the day staff.

Nicola leaned back on the pillows and wondered how she would face another day. It wasn't just the fire and everyone seemed to know it. It was the loss of her father, the questions she had had to answer when the police came, the fury of her father's partner who had come without permission and had to be ordered out by the doctor. Yes, it was everything else.

She looked out of the window, watching the start of another beautiful summer day. It was barely six and the hours of the rest of the day seemed to stretch in front of her bleakly. The sun was edging its way round to her window and the bright rays brought back the heat, the fierce licking flames. She had lost everything, but she was alive although, at the moment, it didn't really feel like that. Everything seemed to be drained from her, her energy sapped away and she felt empty inside.

The bitter hurt was the thing she couldn't really face. They said her father had started the fire himself, a deliberate act to solve his financial problems. The police had been sure of it and so had his partner, Clive Benson. Grief had given way to something much deeper, a sense of betrayal that had left her feeling hopeless.

The electronics firm of Rogers & Benson had been doing well until the past two years, but they had suffered just like any other firm in the hard times and nobody had really known the true state of affairs except her father. Kevin Rogers was the brains of the whole firm—he knew computers, he managed the contracts—and Clive Benson had been pointing that out to her pretty ferociously when the doctor had come in and taken one furious look before ordering him out.

Her father had lost his own life getting her out of the blazing house, but she could not face the fact that he had started the whole thing knowing she was sleeping upstairs. He had put her at risk, destroyed everything around her, and not in any panic-stricken way. It had been planned. Only the week before, he had been checking the insurance on the house. Payment from that would have given the firm a much-needed boost, enough, in all probability, to put it back on its feet.

The police had told her all this, and although they had been kind and gentle, reminding her that people under stress acted without thought, reminding her too that her father had saved her without any consideration for his own life, the stark fact remained and would always remain: he had known she was there, asleep and defenceless. Nicola couldn't face that.

There had just been the two of them because she could barely remember her mother and they had been closer than anyone else she knew. She had worked with him, planned her university course to fit in with the firm so that she could be an even greater part of his life. Now, the truth had left her with nothing but shattered dreams. Her past and her future seemed to have been consumed as the home she had lived in had been consumed. She didn't even possess any clothes. Everything she owned had gone up in terrifying flames and black smoke, taking with it all her past. The firm would be wound up and creditors would fight over the remains like dogs over a bone.

'How are you today, Miss Rogers?'

The doctor came in with the day sister and looked at her sympathetically. They were all looking like that, even the police had looked like that, and it only made her feel worse, as if she would never get back her old fighting spirit.

'I think I'm better.' She managed a smile, but he looked very doubtful.

'Well, you didn't actually get burned, not even your hair.' His glance moved over her thick golden hair, now tied back with a ribbon that one of the nurses had produced for her. 'The smoke, though, was another matter. A few minutes more...'

He didn't continue and she was grateful. A few minutes more and she would not have recovered from the effects of breathing in the smoke. A few minutes more and her father's gallant act would have been pointless.

'I was lucky,' Nicola said quietly. The sister glanced at both of them, murmured incoherently and then went out. Nicola steeled herself for bad news. It was this particular doctor who had been left to tell her about her father. He seemed to get the worst jobs and now it looked as if he had another unpleasant task, because Sister had done her disappearing act before when there had been trouble to relate.

'John Gregory has been your doctor for a long time, I believe?' he murmured, and Nicola looked up at him with startled green eyes.

'For as long as I can remember. He came to see me the other day.'

'So I understand.' He smiled a little uneasily. 'Not many of that sort left, who follow their patients halfway across the county and want daily reports.'

'He was my—my father's friend, too.' Nicola looked down at her pale, slender fingers, wondering where this was leading, wishing he would just say what he had to say and not ramble along like this.

'I see. I thought it was just this old family doctor thing—a disappearing breed. Of course, now that you've told me about... Naturally, it explains things.'

'What things?' Nicola looked up at him a little wildly. Didn't he realise that he was driving her into a panic when she had enough of those to last for the rest of her life?

'Apparently, Dr Gregory has been arranging your future,' he said, picking up her agitation.

'He's what?' It was so unexpected that Nicola almost jerked to attention. She would have to sort out her own future, and nobody knew that better than she did herself.

'He must know a lot about you—of course that would be because of his friendship with your father. It appears that he decided to contact your relatives...'

'I haven't got any,' Nicola informed him in a puzzled voice, and he raised his eyebrows and looked at her as if she was being secretive.

'You must have relatives, because he's unearthed them and they're coming to get you.'

She just stared at him, unable to speak. What relatives? As far as she knew there was one only, her father's sister who lived in America. She had never seen her and there had been no sort of correspondence: no birthday cards, no Christmas cards. The woman might very well be dead by now. Even if she wasn't, she was a stranger!

'There must be some mistake,' Nicola said shakily. 'There's an aunt, but she lived in America the last we heard and that was when I was a little girl. Even if she's still alive, she won't want to see me. She didn't even keep in touch with my father and they were brother and sister. I think Dr Gregory has made some sort of mistake. She couldn't be coming to get me.'

'He didn't say anything about a woman. He said that *they* were coming. At any rate, I expect Dr Gregory will be here today to tell you all about it. He seemed to be very pleased with himself.'

He went out and Nicola could quite understand why the sister had slipped away. It seemed that her life was going to become more muddled than ever. John Gregory was an old dear, but he had made a very bad move with this. She wasn't going to any unknown relatives and asking them to have her was an impertinence that made her squirm with embarrassment.

When Dr Gregory came he certainly looked pleased with himself and Nicola didn't know what to say, how to bring up the subject.

'I've got you all sorted out, Nicola!' he announced proudly when he had watched her closely, walked round her until she felt worried and insisted upon listening to her lungs himself.

'I—I wish you hadn't...' she began, but he interrupted cheerfully.

'Rot! You've lost everything. You haven't even got the clothes you stand up in, as they say. No home, no job, no future...'

'I'll make my own future,' Nicola informed him, doing some interrupting of her own. 'I know what you've done and I'm astonished. I just don't have any relatives.'

'Oh! Been talking has he?' Dr Gregory looked very disappointed that his bombshell was not to be a glorious surprise. 'I might have known. As to relatives, you do have them, my dear. They live in California and they'll be here to get you tomorrow.'

'I can't go!' Nicola said in some agitation. 'I won't go! They can't possibly want me. I'm not an orphaned child. I'm twenty-four years old and well able to take care of myself.'

'When you're better, Nicola,' he said quietly. 'So you didn't get burned and the smoke damage is just about cleared, but you've had a shock that will take a long time to go. You need care for quite a few months and going out to California will be a total break from everything. You must go. In any case, they're coming for you and I've explained everything.'

'Oh, what will they think?' she muttered half to herself. 'I don't know them, they don't know me, it's impossible to even think about it. They'll feel obliged to do it,' she proclaimed, looking up at Dr Gregory with a good deal of distress on her face. 'People do all sorts of things that they don't really want to. They let themselves be talked into it and I know how persuasive you can be.'

'Hush, my dear. I didn't have to do any persuading at all.' He sat beside her on the bed, taking her hand. 'I spoke to your aunt and told her the whole story. The idea of collecting you was entirely hers. She wants to do it. Just relax and let things take their course. A few weeks in California and you'll feel more like your old self, more able to face things.'

'Will I be travelling on Concorde?' Nicola asked, suddenly angry that life was being arranged for her. 'Do you think they'll let me fly there wearing my hospital nightie?'

'That's better.' He looked pleased, happily ignoring her anger. 'That sounds a bit more like the old Nicola. When you get that sparky temper back you'll be ready to make your own way with things. Meantime, just let them spoil you.'

When he had gone, Nicola sat back to assess this latest shock. So far she hadn't really done much thinking about her future, not even letting her mind dwell on the fact that she was not even wearing her own nightie. Now, with the prospect of very important visitors, she wondered what to do. She didn't own a thing. She had a little money in the bank, but she didn't even have her cheque-book or credit card. They had gone with everything else.

It looked as if she would have to face unknown relatives as she was. She got carefully out of bed and went to the bathroom, staring at herself worriedly, barely recognising the face that looked back at her. All her colour seemed to have gone. Her thick, golden hair was almost lifeless, her long green eyes too big in a pale face. She looked nondescript, washed out and dejected.

Not that it mattered, because she wasn't going anywhere at all with anyone at all. When they let her leave hospital she would go to the bank and then go to a small, inexpensive hotel. She had already mentioned clothes to the night sister. It was summer. All she needed was a dress, undies, shoes and some sort of bag. Sister had promised to look into things. She didn't really need anyone at all, and her lips drooped when she became aware that she was bitterly telling herself that she would never trust anyone again.

Later, when the night staff came on, the sister arrived looking very pleased with herself.

'I got your things,' she announced in a satisfied voice. 'Just what you said you wanted, and I added a little jacket of mine that I'm not going to need any more. You can keep it,' she insisted firmly when Nicola made protesting sounds. 'It might just be chilly. As to the rest, you can pay me when you've sorted things out with your bank.'

It was very kind of her and Nicola said so, but when she looked at the bill she was a little stunned. She was used to being expensively dressed, and these things had cost so little that she couldn't quite work out how they had been bought. Still, it didn't matter. She just had to get herself out of here and she would manage somehow. She didn't know what was going to happen to the firm, but there would be something to come to her and, until then, the money she had in the bank would have to last. She needed a job, too, but she was sufficiently realistic to know that she couldn't cope with one for a couple of weeks at least.

It was quite frightening next day to be waiting to meet people she had never seen before when she knew they would be here only because they felt a duty. She didn't want anyone to feel a duty towards her. She didn't want anyone at all. None of her friends had been to visit her and that hurt, too. Boyfriends had not been part of her world since university. Her world had been the firm and the great interest she had in electronics, all of it inspired by her father. She had often worked with him late into the night. It had left little time for a life of her own and now she felt completely lost.

It only made things worse that she would have to face strangers who would probably smile and make all the right noises, but would really feel resentful that duty had dragged them to England to take on a responsibility. Not that she had any intention of going with them. She could not pretend any more. Her interest in everything had died and it suited her to be here in the quiet hospital room, cut off from the world.

She was very tired today. Twice in the night she had been awakened by the sister rushing in when she had screamed and tried to shake off the terror of the nightmare. It seemed that it would never go and now she was staring at the door, dreading seeing the people who would come through it.

There were clouds in the blue sky and she thought of the jacket that sister had brought for her. Maybe she would need it, but not today. They were reluctant to let her go, the doctor saying that she should stay for another two days at least, and she was very glad. It would serve as a barrier against her relatives. Maybe they wouldn't want to stay until she could go? It would give them an excuse without any embarrassment.

Waiting tired her even more and soon after lunch, when nobody at all had appeared, Nicola fell into a restless sleep, half sitting up in bed, her face exhausted and her hair spread out over the white pillows like strands of spun gold where the sunlight caught it in fitful beams.

'I'm not at all sure that she could face a long journey yet.' The sound of the doctor's voice penetrated her sleep, but Nicola did not open her eyes. It was purely instinctive because she was aware of a difference in the room, something in the air, and she knew at once that they had come, the people she dreaded seeing. 'Sister tells me that twice in the night Miss Rogers had nightmares. It's not unusual, but there's really no way of knowing when this sort of thing is going to stop. It was a horrendous experience and, although she may look unscathed, she is by no means recovered.'

'She doesn't look exactly unscathed to me. I don't imagine she usually looks so worn out.'

Nicola tensed at the sound of a voice she had never heard before. It was deep, subtly American and it appeared to carry a lot of authority. She had not been mistaken. They were here. She had to face them, and she would have felt more capable of facing them if she had been in her own clothes, sitting up and wide awake. Even her hair would be tousled. She felt like staying with her eyes closed, hiding, but she knew she could not—they had to be faced now and told that she would not leave England.

She opened her eyes and found two eyes watching her intently, dark eyes in a deeply tanned face. There was no pity on the face either and she was instantly grateful because she didn't want any. His hair was very dark, too, and the authority she had heard in his voice was not a mistake. She could see it on his face, in his eyes and in the firm set of his mouth. She could see it in the way he looked straight at her, summing her up coolly with no apologies.

'Oh, you're awake.' The doctor said it with some relief. He looked a little uneasy, as if talking to the dark-haired man had not been exactly a pleasure, and Nicola assumed at once that the doctor had been informed that there was no possibility of her being taken to America or anywhere else. 'If you're feeling reasonably all right, I'll leave you to have a talk with your cousin,' the doctor went on, edging himself towards the door.

'Thank you. I feel perfectly fine.' Nicola smiled up at him, prolonging the time left before she would have to talk to the man who was making her very uncomfortable without doing anything at all. She was very much aware of power, his height, his wealthy appearance and his coolly handsome face. He stood silently, watching her, and it was hard not to panic.

As the door closed behind the doctor she could no longer put off the inevitable and she turned wary green eyes on her visitor who stood tall and rather intimidating by the bed. As it was, any words died in her throat and she just sat there staring at him apprehensively. How was she going to inform him that she had no intention of leaving with him? He had come all the way across the Atlantic to fetch her, unless he had simply come to say no?

Nicola just went on staring at him, unable to think of anything to say and he looked back, completely unsmiling.

'I'm not your cousin at all,' he assured her, looking down at her with narrow-eyed concentration, 'unless there's such a thing as a stepcousin. I'm Blake Anderson. How are you, Nicola?'

The name fitted him perfectly and rang some sort of bell at the back of her mind, but she was too flustered to dwell on that. He looked tremendously tall as he stood there, almost towering over her and there was a lithe, athletic power about him that made her more nervous still. He seemed to be in his thirties, perhaps thirty-five or -six, but it was impossible to tell, really. There was nothing easygoing about him, she was sure of that.

'I'm quite well, thank you,' she said huskily, pulling herself up in bed and making herself face him.

Instantly he helped her, his hand coming beneath her arm, lifting her as if she had no weight at all, and before she could settle back he had the pillows fluffed up and behind her head.

'You're very polite, Nicola, but not exactly truthful,' he murmured, swinging a chair forward and sitting to face her. 'You look anything but well. Apparently you could leave tomorrow, but that might be unwise, according to the doctor.'

She was in something of a dilemma, knowing that he was edging round to telling her that they couldn't have her. It reminded her that he was the only one here and she realised that she had allowed herself to be a little mesmerised by him. The relatives she had dreaded had not materialised, but there was a very powerful emissary in their place.

'I—I expected to see my aunt,' she began and his face tightened as if she had said something wrong.

'Mary is not fit to travel, certainly not this far.'

'Mary?' She looked at him with a puzzled expression on her face and he stared at her impatiently.

'Your aunt. I'm afraid you'll have to make do with me. I had to be in England, in any case, and collecting you myself was an ideal solution. Mary stayed at home.'

Nicola could see that she had partially antagonised him. She hadn't even remembered her aunt's name, but it was not surprising. She hadn't heard it since she was a little girl. He must think she wanted to be surrounded by a lot of sympathetic people. He was talking about collecting her, too, and she had to put an end to this right away. It was so obviously a duty and she was very wary of him already. Even if she had been thinking of going, the sight of him would have scared her off.

'I think I can save both of us a lot of embarrassment,' she said quietly. 'I had no idea that Dr Gregory had been in touch with my aunt. He never mentioned it to me until he had everything arranged. I don't need any help at all. I'm not a child, I'm twenty-four. In—in any case, I don't want to go to America so there's really no need for you to feel obliged to——'

'I don't feel obliged to do anything,' he informed her in a very hardened voice, cutting in on her husky explanation. 'Mary asked me to get you and I'm here to do just that.'

'I'm sorry, but I just don't want to go.' Nicola decided that it was time to be firm, to let him know that she was in control. 'I don't know my aunt and I've no intention of being a burden to anyone.'

'You'll be no burden to Mary,' he said shortly. 'I won't allow it.' She opened her mouth to speak, but he cut her off by raising his hand for silence as if he was quite used to obedience. 'Let me explain the situation. Your Aunt Mary is my stepmother and I'm particularly fond of her. She's not exactly frail, but her life is very much curtailed because of an accident several years ago. This doctor friend of yours has got her highly excited about the prospect of seeing her niece. She's waiting for you. She wants to see you.' He pinned her with hard, dark eyes, concentrated power thrown at her. 'You'll go, Nicola, believe me.'

She just looked at him blankly. She didn't know him at all, but he thought he could tell her what to do and when to do it. He hadn't even considered her wishes. He was watching her with peculiar intensity and she had the impression of some dark, ferocious animal, silently tensed, waiting to pounce if she made a wrong move.

He would have to be treated cautiously and she realised that. At one time she would have told him sharply to keep out of her affairs, but she wasn't up to that now and, in any case, he had come a long way to get her. She didn't want to be unfair and ungrateful, but she wasn't going anywhere with him. Just walking down the corridor beside him would be a harrowing experience.

'Look,' she began carefully. 'My father and his sister never even wrote to each other. I'd even forgotten that I had an aunt. She can't possibly want to have me in her house.'

'My house,' he corrected coldly, alarming her even more. 'Mary lives with me and I'd move heaven and earth to make her happy. Right now, she wants you, and that's exactly what she's going to get.'

'Don't I have any say in the matter?' Nicola looked at him with astonished green eyes and he stood, swinging the chair away as he began to pace about with his hands in his pockets.

'This doctor person—Gregory—told Mary all about you and she told me. Let's run through your options—not that you have any,' he added darkly, shooting a piercing look at her. 'Mary wants you and you're going. But on the off-chance that I have an attack of conscience, we'll consider your alternatives. You've lost your home, your job and your belongings. I'm told that you've been very ill and that you're still suffering from shock to a great extent. What do you intend to do on an immediate basis?'

'I—I'll go to a small hotel and, when I feel a bit better, I'll get some work and...'

'That's a load of rubbish and you know it,' he snapped. 'You need help, even if you're too stubborn to admit it. Help is waiting for you.'

'I'm grateful but...'

'Nobody needs gratitude. Mary's not the sort to expect it and I'm just the courier. Common sense would be a hell of a sight better than gratitude.' He looked at her sceptically. 'Maybe she'll be disappointed in her new-found niece. In that case, you can escape and come back to England. In the meantime, at least you can get a bit of sun. You sure look as if you need it.'

His attitude had wound her up tightly inside. He was clearly quite used to getting his own way and she could see that he was prepared to argue all day and night if need be. He had made his mind up without ever having seen her, as if she was of no importance. Aunt Mary wanted her and that was what was going to happen.

'I won't be made to feel guilty,' Nicola said in a trembling voice. 'I won't be bullied, either.'

'Oh, yes, you will, Nicola,' he informed her softly. 'I came to get you and I'm not leaving without you. Give in now because you will—finally. Everyone gives in finally.'

'Because you harass them,' Nicola pronounced. He had made her feel more tired than ever and she felt choked up with warring feelings, guilt, frustration and a certain amount of fright.

'Probably. I'm prepared to do anything at all to get what I want,' he agreed. 'Right now, I want you on a plane and heading back to California and your aunt. That is exactly what you'll do.'

'I can't even leave hospital yet,' Nicola whispered, dropping her head to hide the tears that were suddenly glazing her eyes.

'Leave all that to me.' He came back to stand by the bed and then sat beside her. 'You need looking after.' Lean brown fingers tilted her face and his dark eyes noted her struggle with tears. 'You may not know your aunt, but she's all you've got. It's a big house. You'll have plenty of privacy, a place of your own if you want to have a good cry.' There was a cruel twist to his lips and it stiffened Nicola sufficiently to still any tears.

'I don't cry!' she informed him sharply.

'Maybe it's time you did,' he countered drily. 'A few more tears may mean a few less nightmares.' He stood abruptly and gazed down at her uncompromisingly. 'I'll be here to get you tomorrow afternoon. I'll deal with the hospital right now.'

'In all probability they won't want to take the responsibility of letting me go just yet,' Nicola pointed out quickly, hanging on to the hope of escaping him although she had already admitted at the back of her mind that everything he had said was sensible and true. 'You said yourself that it wasn't a good idea.'

'Maybe they won't have any choice,' he murmured sceptically. 'As to what I said, I've changed my mind. You look as if you might give some thought to getting away through the window. I'll deal with the hospital and I'll take the responsibility. I'm quite used to it. One slip of a girl isn't going to make much difference to me.'

He simply nodded to her curtly as he left and Nicola stared at the closed door with everything inside her in a turmoil. He was so tall, so tough and powerful that there seemed to be an emptiness to the room now that he had gone. At any time he would have been formidable. Right now, she just couldn't cope with him. He had left her trembling and anxious. What would it be like living in his house?

'Was that your boyfriend at last?' One of the nurses came in with nothing on her mind but gossip and Nicola almost shuddered.

'He's—er—my cousin.' It saved a lot of explanations and she had too much to think about to go into any sort of detail. She had to work out how to defy him and it wasn't easy in her present position.

'Well, *he's* a man and a half if ever I saw one. I never noticed him visiting before.'

'He's just come from America,' Nicola murmured vaguely, her mind on other things entirely. 'It's my—my cousin Blake, Blake Anderson.'

'Blake Anderson?' The nurse came slowly to the bed as if she had been lured there by the name. 'The real Blake Anderson?'

'I expect so,' Nicola muttered vaguely, coming out of her cloudy thoughts. 'He looked real enough to me.' In fact he had looked much too real. He had left an impression of intense dominance behind him that even now lingered in the room.

'He'll be here for the première, then, but I expect you know that?'

'The première?' Nicola gave the nurse her full attention. The bell was starting to ring again in her mind, but she couldn't quite believe it.

'*Cold Justice*! You know! It opens in London tomorrow night. It's a pity you won't be fit enough to go with him. I'd give anything to go to one of those glamorous affairs. Fancy you forgetting that!' She suddenly went very quiet and looked at Nicola with pity. 'Listen to me, rambling on when you've had so much trouble. It's not surprising that you forgot.'

Nicola tried not to think about it until she was alone again and then she was almost too scared to let her mind dwell on it at all. Blake Anderson! No wonder he looked powerful. No wonder he had left such a feeling of force behind him. He was one of the most famous film directors in the world and he had a reputation for complete ruthlessness.

Any actor who disagreed with him was out, no matter what their status. He chose his own stories, did his own editing and drove everyone to exhaustion until he had everything as he wanted it. He had never made a film that was anything but a money-spinner and it was quality that drew the audiences. Most of the films were thrillers, hard and uncompromising, just like Blake Anderson.

Nicola sat stunned. Of course the name had rung a bell; it should have, for she had read about him several times. He was always doing something harsh and unfeeling. And she was planning to defy him! Just the thought of him left her feeling weak and inadequate and now she knew why. He was very fond of Aunt Mary and Aunt Mary wanted her there. Her chances of escape seemed very remote.

CHAPTER TWO

'WELL, you're going, then?' When the night sister came on she was looking at Nicola in an entirely different way.

'Am I?' Nicola felt a shiver run over her skin. The inevitability of it was so overwhelming that she had actually stopped thinking about it altogether.

'You know you are! Fancy never telling me that you had such a famous cousin. The whole hospital is seething with the news and me the last to know.'

She looked very frosty and Nicola couldn't come up with a ready excuse. It was pointless to say that she had not known about her famous relative or to say that he wasn't really a relative at all. Nobody was going to believe her now.

'I wasn't sure if I could go tomorrow,' Nicola murmured, trying to get off the subject of Blake Anderson and her slight claim to fame. 'The doctor said...'

'Oh, Mr Anderson has assured him that you'll have enough luxury around you to make up for anything you'll miss from here,' Sister sniffed. 'Apparently he pointed out sarcastically that there are doctors in America too. I can see where he got that reputation from.'

'He—he's a little uncompromising,' Nicola offered guiltily, and Sister nodded in agreement.

'I just hope he's going to be sympathetic when you have your nightmares,' she said coolly. 'I won't be there to run in to you and wake you up.'

'Perhaps I won't have any more,' Nicola ventured, and that gained her a very sceptical look. Without words, Sister gave the impression that, with Blake Anderson

22

there, the nightmares were probably going to be permanent.

'I'm sorry I didn't tell you,' Nicola said, remembering the sister's kindness. 'I—I forgot.'

'It's all right.' Professional training and sympathy wiped out the sister's annoyance and she patted Nicola's hand. 'No wonder you forget, the things you've faced. I hope you'll be all right with that man.' She looked very dubious and Nicola felt exactly the same.

When Nicola finally went to sleep she had worn herself out with plans that had fallen flat even before they were properly worked out. She was at his mercy. She seemed to be at everyone's mercy at the moment. It wouldn't last. In the end her real character would surface but, for now, she was like a leaf tossed by a storm and Blake Anderson was at the centre of it, dark and ruthless, power-housing her into something she just didn't want to do. She had met him only once, but he seemed to have a hold on her life that could not be shaken off. She could remember every detail of his face, every hard glance from those dark eyes. He was as real as if he still stood irritably by her bed.

The next day, the nurses couldn't seem to get her ready fast enough and Nicola was dressed and waiting long before Blake came. She assumed that they didn't want any sort of confrontation with him and she could only sympathise. If she had not felt exactly the same she would not now be waiting there reluctantly, planning to visit an aunt she had never seen and didn't want to see.

She had to admit that the clothes she wore were pretty awful. They looked even worse now that she had them on than they had done in the packages, but she didn't dwell on the fact. She had only given vague ideas to the sister and she was too tired and too uptight to bother now. In any case, it was astonishing how vulnerable she felt in ordinary clothes. The hospital nightie and robe had been a sort of refuge, the small room a shell that had protected her since the fire, and she had willingly curled herself into that protection.

Now she was about to face the world again but, worse than that, she was about to face a man who had a reputation for inflexible behaviour, a man who lived by rigid rules that he set himself and forced on everyone else. Since his visit, his name seemed to be uppermost in everyone's mind. Nicola heard it muttered on many occasions, sometimes with a sort of awe that attached itself to the glamorous and sometimes with an irritation that she readily recognised. He had left her with similar feelings and she dreaded seeing him again.

Even without the traumatic events that had shaped her life recently, even if she had been her old self, she would have found Blake Anderson too difficult to manage. He was completely outside her understanding, a ready-made adversary for anyone with even slightly sensitive emotions. He would give no quarter at any time and she knew that very surely.

It was well into the afternoon before he came and, by that time, Nicola was feeling quite ill again, her nervous energy drained away by waiting and worrying. He just strode into the room without any warning and she came to her feet as if she had received an order, standing there looking at him in a trapped manner.

He gave her one sceptical glance, noting her nervous stance, and then his eyes fastened on her dress with a great deal of astounded intensity.

'What the hell is that?' he demanded harshly, looking her up and down slowly. 'It looks as if you got it from a paper bag in a back alley.'

There was an insolent irritation in his manner, a cool contempt and Nicola's cheeks flushed with embarrassment as she looked at him resentfully.

'The night sister got it for me. It was very good of her. I don't own anything at all now. I lost all my clothes in...'

'Sure,' he interrupted impatiently. 'We'll deal with the clothes later. Let's get going.'

She hadn't been too bothered about the dress until he'd looked at her like that, but now Nicola felt like a monstrous oddity. He had made her feel bizarre, abnormal, and she had never been so aware of her own body as she felt at that moment. She had a wild inclination to cover herself up, to run into the bathroom and lock the door, and she didn't know how she would be capable of walking out of the hospital with him. Whatever small amount of confidence she had was wiped out by that one glance and those harshly contemptuous words.

As there was no case to carry, Blake simply turned to the door after a glance round the room and she stared at him in frustration. Not only was he going to order her about, he was going to set a time limit on her every move. She knew that she had to assert herself straight away before he got the idea that she would simply obey when he ordered

'I have to call at my bank,' she informed him in as firm a voice as she could summon up. 'I owe the night sister for these things and I have to arrange for a new cheque-book and card and...'

'How much do you need for the sister?' he snapped, glancing at her briefly. 'We'll leave the money now. No stopping at the bank. I have to get back.'

'I pay for my own things,' Nicola said sharply, standing right where she was and looking at him stubbornly. 'I have to go to the bank because I have no money at all. In any case, if you think I'm going to America looking like this...'

'I'm glad it's not normal,' he grated, his dark eyes skimming her slender figure again. He glanced up at her irritably. 'You're not going to America right now. The getting back I have to do is to my hotel. I'm busy and you look as if you need to get your feet up. Let's go!'

This time, he opened the door wide, stood aside and looked at her coldly and Nicola found herself obeying the sharp command. Of course he would be busy. There was this première.

'I'll have to go to the bank tomorrow, then,' she insisted, and he took her arm in a very uncompromising way, pushing doors open along the hospital corridor and urging her forward.

'We'll see.' It was clearly the only answer she was going to get and Nicola found her lost temper trying very hard to surface. If he thought she was going to America without money and clothes, to be left at his mercy and peered at by people she had never seen before, he had another think coming. When they got outside, into the open air and some amount of privacy she would make a stand, let him know she was not to be ordered about like this.

'What's her name?' As they came to the main reception desk, Blake stopped and snapped out the question.

'Who?' Nicola looked at him in a daze. He was like a tightly controlled storm and she had the feeling that at any moment he was capable of exploding into black violence and overwhelming her.

'The sister! The one you owe a minor fortune to.' He cast another scathing glance at her attire. 'Whatever it cost, you've been robbed. She stole it from a museum.'

'Sister Bennett!' Nicola told him crossly, her face pink again. 'And I told you I had no alternative but to...'

'How much?' he snapped.

When she told him the amount, one dark brow rose ironically, amusement colouring his contempt.

'It came in a gold box?'

'There were other—things,' Nicola informed him, her cheeks burning with embarrassment. To her relief he turned away, going to the desk to leave the money to be passed to the sister and, when he turned back, his mood had very subtly changed.

'Come on,' he said softly. 'Let's get out of here. You need a nice stiff brandy and a nice comfortable bed.'

She could only agree with him. If this was how he intended to go on she would need more than a stiff brandy. He quite understood that she felt weak too. She wondered how he would behave when she felt better? Not that it mattered. When she felt better he would not have such an easy victim beside him. She gave him a baleful look and, as he was glancing at her at the same time, he noticed.

'Something troubling you, Nicola?' he enquired sardonically, and she looked away quickly, not feeling exactly up to a battle at the moment.

'Not at all. I feel a little dazed, but I'm sure it will pass.'

He gave her a very searching look, but said nothing and Nicola kept quiet. She was still weighing up her chances of getting out of this. At the moment she felt incapable of defending herself, but perhaps she would feel better in the morning. If she did, she would just walk out and leave him to order somebody else around. He was impossible, hateful and hurtful. She had a terrible desire to attack him physically, a feeling she had never had before with anyone.

He had a car, not the gleaming American limousine she had vaguely imagined, but a dark Mercedes, and when she was inside and he came round to drive away she ventured a question that had been right at the front of her mind since he had called for her.

'Where are you staying?' she asked quietly.

'London. The Savoy.'

'So—so where will I be staying?' Nicola wanted to know anxiously.

'With me!' He turned his head to give her an exasperated look. 'I've got a lot to fit in while I'm here and I can hardly be racing from one hotel to another, keeping an eye on you. I'm supposed to be looking after you until I hand you over to Mary and I intend to do it in the easiest way possible.'

'I don't need looking after,' Nicola began stormily, annoyed to be spoken of as if she was a child to be 'handed over'. 'I'm quite capable of taking care of myself!'

'When you're better,' he agreed abruptly, after a keen glance at her annoyed face. 'Until then you stay with me. No choice allowed!'

'You've already booked a room for me?'

'I've got a suite. Two bedrooms and a sitting-room. You'll be perfectly all right there. I can get about my affairs and see to you at the same time.'

It quelled Nicola's rising temper and she sat in silence, watching the traffic as they sped down the motorway. It was all so staggering. Right out of the blue she had a relative and a very fierce man with a reputation for getting his own way was ruthlessly taking her where she didn't want to go. She didn't have a thing of her own and after his looks and comments she felt very embarrassed about her present clothes.

It would have been bad enough going to some small hotel in her home town, going to her bank and getting a taxi, wearing the things she had on. Now she was about to be introduced to the Savoy. They would drive up in a Mercedes and he would get out and drag her in by the arm as if he had found her wandering about abandoned in an undesirable back street.

'What will they think?' she muttered aloud, her voice filled with anxiety.

'They'll think I'm eccentric. I can live with it.' She looked across at him and saw a twisted smile quirking at his lips. He probably could live with it as he quite obviously cared nothing for people and their opinions. He wasn't at all worried about whether she could live with it or not.

'No doubt they'll be intrigued,' Nicola snapped. 'You can tell them I'll be perfect for a bit-part in one of your films. I can be a poor down-at-heel servant girl.'

'Ah! So you've been looking into my background,' he surmised scathingly. 'Don't worry. You'll not be seeing anything of the world I live in. You're with Mary.'

'I did not look into your background,' Nicola informed him sharply. 'It was all pushed down my throat by shivering nurses who were enthralled by your fame. I had a hard time getting out of the fact that I hadn't shouted loudly that my cousin was *the* Blake Anderson!'

'I'm not your cousin, Nicola,' he pointed out darkly. 'I'm no relative at all. What I am, though, is the guy who intends to get you to your aunt. Don't try any tricks. I can almost hear your brain working. You're with me. The next person you're with—is Mary.'

'She'll be startled,' Nicola muttered, looking down at her unfashionable dress, subdued by the powerful wave of authority that seemed to be almost thrown at her.

'By the time she sees you, you won't look like that,' he promised grimly. 'We'll deal with the clothes tomorrow.'

'I could have dealt with my own clothes if you'd been willing to stop at my bank...'

'I know what you should be wearing,' he said inflexibly. 'I'll deal with you tomorrow. Tonight, I'm busy.'

'The première,' Nicola muttered, and he looked across at her with the wide ferocious grin of a tiger.

'The première,' he agreed. 'You want to go? I don't have a partner. Go with me in that dress and I guarantee that next week it will be a new fashion, people ringing you to ask where they can get a copy.'

'It must be a great burden to be so important,' Nicola snapped with a sarcasm of her own.

'Oh, it is,' he assured her drily. 'I can't sleep nights.'

He got on with the driving and said nothing more and Nicola decided that for the moment she was out-classed. He was too much for her and he had a very great advantage over her, too. He didn't care at all what people thought. That was one of his undesirable traits.

So far she hadn't heard of or discovered for herself any traits that were *not* undesirable. He was a hard, powerful man and he looked as if he enjoyed being exactly what he was. Her Aunt Mary must be similar or she wouldn't be able to live with him. It was going to be terrible. Nicola began to sink into gloom and he never noticed because he never even glanced in her direction at all. She had no doubt that she was quite unimportant, no more than a piece of extra luggage.

Her anxiety grew once they were in London. She hardly noticed the traffic because she was dreading the coming ordeal. By now she was certain that she looked ridiculous and shabby. People would stare at her. They might even laugh. She wanted to beg to be taken somewhere else, but one look at Blake's face was enough to still that thought.

When they walked into the hotel, people seemed to spring at them from every corner. Instantly, Blake was the centre of attention, the focus of all eyes.

'Several messages for you, Mr Anderson.' The receptionist darted forward and thrust notes at him as he swept past with Nicola in tow. Blake just nodded, grasped the notes and kept going. Nicola was too worried about her appearance to even take a deep breath and her legs started trembling. She felt weak, realising quite clearly that she would have been much better in hospital and still in bed.

'Can you give us a smile, Mr Anderson? A few words?'

'Can you look straight at the camera, Mr Anderson?'

To her horror there were newsmen, a small crowd of them. There seemed to be a whole battery of cameras, but Blake was not stopping. He gave a sort of cold smile that might or might not have been amusement.

'Catch me later,' he suggested. His voice was taut, very American and Nicola knew he could not afford to be seen with her. He was too important. It all added to her wretched feelings and she almost dived into the lift, feeling momentarily secure when the door closed on them. Blake had got her through that crowd as if she was invisible. Even so, she felt the strain now and her face was paler than ever. She had been feeling ill and weak even before they set off from the hospital. Now she felt much worse.

'I never expected that,' she murmured, almost in a whisper.

'It's one of the hazards of life,' he grated, leaning back and drumming his fingers impatiently against the side of the lift.

'Will—will they be wondering why I'm...?'

'You're having suburban thoughts?' he enquired in a harshly taunting voice. 'Don't worry, they'll never even begin to suspect that you're with me.' The dark eyes swept over her again and Nicola could have wept with shame and frustration, with tiredness and the feeling of being utterly helpless and shabby.

He knew that she had lost everything. He knew she had had a most horrendous experience that had left her disorientated, adrift and lonely and yet he showed no sort of mercy. After the glance and the cruel words, he never looked at her again and she felt like a parcel that was being delivered by a very reluctant go-between who was far above that sort of thing. He would probably have preferred to send her, labelled and secured with the luggage, cash on delivery.

'I'm not going with you to America!'

She stood in the centre of the sitting-room when they arrived and made the statement with apparent calm. In fact she was shaking, not only because she was just out of hospital, but because everything seemed to be piling up on her. She knew she could not take much more of this mental battering and saw no reason why she should.

Blake just walked across to her and began to remove her jacket. He never looked at her face. His eyes were simply on his task and the jacket was off before she could react. He threw it in the general direction of a chair, picked her up and walked through into one of the bedrooms.

'What are you doing?' Nicola's voice was a strangled sound and she clutched at him anxiously.

'I'm warding off disaster! Later, you can cry your eyes out, but right now I'm too busy to cope with you. Bed, Nicola!' He swept the cover aside and put her on the bed, pulling off her shoes and tossing them down with the same careless abandon he had used with the jacket. 'Stay put!' he ordered when she looked up at him with wild eyes. 'The drink comes next.'

He was out of the room before she could manage to speak, but she was ready when he came back in with a glass containing brandy.

'You didn't hear me,' she began tremulously. 'I'm not going to America.'

'I heard you.' He sat beside her on the bed and handed her the glass. 'The fact that I ignored you does not mean that I didn't hear.'

'Ignoring me won't do any good,' she told him shakily. 'I've quite made my mind up. I'm not going.'

Hard fingers tilted her face and he looked very deeply into her eyes for a minute. It was a long, considering look that left Nicola feeling hypnotised again and he kept the pressure up until she was staring back at him helplessly.

'Oh, yes, you are,' he pronounced steadily. 'You're going back with me the day after tomorrow. You're going straight to your Aunt Mary and, until then, you're going to rest, eat and sleep. Now, drink your brandy and have a little snooze. I'll get you fed before I leave for the première.'

He walked out and Nicola stared at the closed door. She had the uneasy conviction that even when she was well, she would find it difficult to deal with Blake Anderson. She sipped the brandy and then lay back, closing her eyes and willing herself to relax.

If he had been at all nice she would have been thankful to stay here and then go with him, just until she felt better. He was not nice, though. He was hateful. She fell asleep with that thought in her mind, frowning at the image of his tanned face that floated before her closed eyes. He was a man she would have to fight and she knew it deep inside.

She slept for two hours and, for once, there were no nightmares. The sleep would probably have lasted longer, but there was a sharp knocking on the bedroom door and, as she struggled up in bed, Blake walked in. He was in evening dress, obviously ready to go out and Nicola stared at him blankly. He was a stranger and seeing him like this brought home the fact very sharply.

The white shirt emphasised his tan and, in evening clothes, he looked quite magnificent. At any time he would have looked striking, but she now realised quite guiltily that if she had seen him in the street she would have been intrigued by his hard good looks, by the way he walked and by the air of arrogant impatience that seemed to cover him like a forbidding cloak. It was astonishing that fate had thrown her in his path at all and more astonishing still that she was actually staying here with him.

Looking at things objectively, she had simply allowed a man she did not know to take her from the safety of the hospital and bring her to his hotel suite. Nobody actually knew where she was. It had all been done on the strength of her relationship to Aunt Mary and Blake Anderson's insistence on being a go-between of an inexorable variety. She had taken his word for everything. She had never spoken to her aunt. Dr Gregory was the only one who had any proof at all of her existence.

'You can change into this,' Blake stated after staring back at her for a second. He tossed a package on to the bed and Nicola looked at it warily. It was a large striped box, tied with white ribbon and it looked as if it had come from some exclusive shop.

'What is it?' She pushed her tousled golden hair back from a face that was still flushed with sleep and glanced at him with deep suspicion.

'Something to sleep in,' he said abruptly, his dark eyes pinning her, glittering and relentless. 'As you had no sort of suitcase and the hospital nightdress was left on your bed, I assumed that you needed night attire.'

'I—I suppose I do,' Nicola muttered charily.

'Well, the dress hasn't improved with sleeping in it,' he ground out, 'and you're hardly in a condition to make it to the shops tonight. Put it on,' he added impatiently when she just stared at him. 'I want to get you fed and settled before I go.'

He walked out and Nicola opened the box with some hesitation. She didn't like the idea of anyone getting clothes for her, especially not this sort of thing. It made her more uneasy than ever and, when she drew from the box a very expensive, silk nightdress in ivory and a matching robe, her face flushed with a mixture of embarrassment and anxiety. Just what had she allowed herself to be bullied into? Uncomfortable thoughts came flooding into her mind.

She was very quick in the shower, her uneasiness making her feel that he may stride back in to hurry her along. All the same she felt better for her sleep and even better after the warm shower. She dried her hair and combed it into smooth silken waves that swung around her shoulders and she began to feel almost human when she slid into the silk nightie and robe.

She didn't quite have the nerve to walk out into the sitting-room, though. She didn't know Blake Anderson at all and it was very different from seeing him at the hospital. There was something just too intimate about wandering in to see him now, wearing a very glamorous nightie and robe.

'Nicola!' He banged uncompromisingly on the bedroom door and she knew he was not about to let her hide until he left. 'Come out! Let's have a look at you.'

It made her gasp with annoyance. He was treating her like a child with a new dressing-gown who had to parade around to show it off. His attitude strengthened her more than anything else could and she marched out with a frown on her face to find him sitting quite comfortably with a whisky glass in his hand. He was all ready to inspect her and she glared at him.

'What's the matter?' he enquired disparagingly after one glance at her flushed and annoyed face. 'Don't they fit?'

'They fit very well, thank you,' Nicola snapped. 'It was kind of you to go and get them.'

'I didn't go and get them,' he assured her drily. 'I rang Reception and got an address. I then rang the shop and had them sent round.'

'Reception? What will they be thinking now?' Nicola asked in an outraged voice, her cheeks going rose-pink.

'Ordinary people don't *think* about people like me,' he pointed out mockingly. 'They expect either eccentricity or diabolical behaviour. In a place like this, they keep their thoughts to themselves.'

It made her feel quite ridiculous and also a little like a shocked maiden aunt. He had a superb way of putting people down, she noted, and another thought crossed her mind and was blurted out before she could stop it.

'How did you know my size?' Her suspicious question had that tiger grin back on his face.

'Well, I didn't sneak in there with a tape measure while you slept.' He stood abruptly and walked to the phone. 'I'll order your meal now.' When she just kept quite still and stared at him uneasily he looked irritated again. 'For God's sake, Nicola!' he snapped. 'I'm watching women all day and every day. It's my job to watch people. Guessing your size was no big deal. I had a rough idea of your height and you seem to be made in the correct proportions.'

Nicola sank back into being a Victorian spinster again. She could see it on his face—a mixture of contempt and impatience and his complete conviction that nobody would even begin to imagine she was with him. He didn't just have a big ego, he was quite god-like and she imagined it was the prolonged impact of fame.

He didn't ask her what she wanted to eat either. She heard him ordering a light meal for one to be served immediately and she just gave up. One thing was for sure, though, she was not about to sit there while some waiter came to serve it. He might very well keep his thoughts to himself, but they would be there all the same.

She silently disappeared into her bedroom and closed the door.

It was not a very good idea, the look on Blake's face as he followed her and simply walked in told her that clearly.

'Will you stop doing this sort of thing?' he ordered irascibly. 'I refuse to stalk after you whenever you decide to slink off.'

'I did not slink off. . .' Nicola began, but his eyes slid over her comprehensively and he gave one of his tight, caustic smiles.

'You've got the equipment for it,' he observed drily. 'Let's get down to some planning. I've got about half an hour before I leave.'

'I don't think it's suitable to talk in my bedroom.' Nicola sounded severe and Blake glowered at her, his dark eyes flashing sparks.

'Then get the hell out of it,' he snapped. 'Or do you want me to roar at you from the other room?' He turned and walked out, muttering under his breath and, once again, she found herself trailing after him—capitulating.

'You,' he pronounced, turning round to point one hard finger at her, 'are going to be a source of constant irritation!'

'I never asked you to come for me,' Nicola said sharply. 'I never asked to be looked after. I don't want any relatives.'

'Mary wants you. That's why I'm here and that's why I'm looking after you. Before I get you to Mary you'll be steady on your feet, dressed correctly and in a better frame of mind.'

'There's nothing wrong with my mind!' Nicola retorted crossly. 'And nobody asked me what *I* want!'

'What you want is a damned good shaking,' he growled. 'Keep on like this and you're likely to get one.'

'*I am not a child*!' Nicola actually raised her voice to a shout and he was across the room in two long strides, his hands like steel on her arms. What he intended to do she did not know, but there was a murderous rage at the back of the dark eyes and Nicola started trembling, not from fear but from the great surge of anger that had made her shout. She just wasn't strong enough for this sort of thing yet.

For a second he glared down at her and then his cruel grip relaxed.

'Don't fight with me until you're better,' he warned, obviously deciding to curb his temper. 'When you're up to it, I'll give you any sort of battle you want. Right now, you're in no state to take me on. Don't try it.' His voice may have eased from rage, but there was a menace behind it that did nothing to calm Nicola's trembling and he suddenly ran his fingers down her cheek, his hard mouth softening into near-amusement. 'In the foolish days of my youth,' he related mockingly, 'I once brought a small, bedraggled kitten home. I washed it, fed it and made it a nice warm bed. It was so utterly grateful that it bit me and gave me a deep scratch. I had to have a damned big injection.'

'I'm germ-free,' Nicola said shakily, understanding the comparison he was making between her and some other ungrateful creature, and he grinned down at her in his first show of genuine amusement.

'That's a relief. You look as if you might bite at any moment. Sit down, Nicola. I want a list of your needs and there's only tomorrow to deal with them.'

'I—I can't actually go out like—like this,' she began worriedly, sinking to the settee and wondering if his contempt for convention would stretch to taking her to Bond Street in a nightie.

'Clothes are no problem,' he announced briskly. 'I've already dealt with that while you slept. In the morning a couple of places are sending round some things for you to try. They're prepared to dress you from the skin out.'

Nicola flushed all over again and he glanced at her with raised brows, her attitude evidently astonishing him. He let it pass though and went on,

'What I need to know is about make-up. What sort do you wear, what do you need? They'll bring bags and shoes, but I need to know the shoe size and I didn't venture into what you put on your face.'

As she hadn't had anything on her face for days, Nicola suddenly felt very drab again, in spite of the glamorous night-wear. It was interesting to find out how the rich and famous lived too. She had visions of page-boys coming in a stream, each carrying boxes on velvet cushions. She gave a subdued giggle and quickly closed her mouth on it as he glanced at her sharply.

'Now what?' he asked suspiciously. 'I've blundered again? You don't wear make-up?'

'Er—yes. I—er—I was just imagining...' She trailed into silence and he sat back and regarded her with narrowed-eyed interest.

'I'm beginning to wonder what Mary will make of you,' he mused quietly. 'You're decidedly odd, aren't you?'

'Americans don't really understand the English,' she assured him and he nodded in agreement.

'Maybe not. American women tend to keep up a sustained force. You attack in short bursts and then subside into feminine trembling. Female guerrilla tactics. I've never met it before. Having you around will be an education.'

'I don't suppose I'll be there for long,' Nicola said hastily. 'You can see that I'm feeling better already.'

'You're not.' He looked at her steadily, his dark, glittering glance running over her. 'You're safe here and

you obviously have a talent for making complications.
Put you out into the world, though, and you would just
fold up and collapse.'

'I wouldn't!' Nicola once again felt the trap closing
and she tried to sound firm and strong.

'You're not going to get the chance,' he murmured
wryly. 'Now let's get back to the things you need,' he
added, glancing at a thin gold watch on his wrist. 'I want
all this sorted before I leave. I'll be on the phone before
you're awake and then we'll get busy.'

It was little use arguing. She had already discovered
that and Nicola gave in, telling him her brand of make-
up and her shoe size. He wrote it down and she was still
a little breathless from her encounter with him when the
meal was served. She had no time to disappear either
and the waiter solicitously held her chair while Blake
stood and watched like a tyrant.

If she didn't eat, the waiter had probably been tipped
to betray her. The food looked good, but she didn't have
much appetite and there was nothing like pressure for
taking even that away. As the waiter left she glanced
rather tragically at Blake and to her surprise he recognised her problem.

'Just eat what you want. Somebody will be back to
collect the things later. They don't punish you for left-
overs.'

Nicola smiled faintly. She hadn't expected that they
would. Punishment seemed to be Blake's forte. Working
for him must be nerve-racking because he looked as if
he would have no patience at all and he looked very
clever, as if he would always be right. She would hate
to be the one to tell him on the rare occasions when he
was wrong.

CHAPTER THREE

THE girl who came to collect the trays smiled at her sympathetically.

'What a pity you're not well when Mr Anderson has a première. He told us he was taking his cousin back with him and that you were ill. Never mind,' she added in a consoling voice, 'you can see it on television, if you like, although I suppose you've already seen the film. It must have been exciting to make.'

Nicola just swallowed her astonishment and smiled weakly. It seemed to be expected of her. She felt a wave of fury at Blake. He had let her worry and be embarrassed about being here and yet he had told them that she was his sick cousin. Why couldn't he have let her know that? And whom had he told? Had he sent a note round to all interested parties?

It was quite clear that she was supposed to be in on this film business. No doubt they thought she was his right-hand man, leaning over and shouting 'Cut!' when he nodded his important head. She paced about the room when the girl had left and simply seethed. He would be preening himself at this important première right now. In spite of herself she switched on the set to watch, finding the channel after a second and seeing the great big cars pulling up outside.

Of course she had heard of the film—who had not?— but she had never expected to be so intimately connected with its director. The stars were just arriving and she could quite see why Blake thought her drab, especially in that awful dress and wearing no make-up. Glamour was stepping out of each car, every one of them with adoring escorts. She knew every face even though she was not an avid cinemagoer.

When Blake came there was a lot of murmuring and he looked none too pleased. Nicola noted that none of the stars came forward for a kiss as she had seen on these occasions before and she became quite intrigued. Blake looked as if this was some sort of imposition. He nodded curtly at the cameras and then walked in, out of sight, people glancing a little nervously after him. Even the way he moved seemed to spell out danger. Once again he looked like a tiger and there was something proud and ferocious about him that warned any likely enthusiasts away.

Nicola switched off and sat back, her mind gnawing away anxiously at the impressions it had just received. Seen at a distance, he looked more forbidding than ever and, once again, she wondered how she had managed to get herself into the position where he had any power over her at all. His presence had almost driven her memories of horror away. It was impossible to ignore him and it was equally impossible to think of anything else whenever he was near.

She went to bed, her thoughts tossing between the terror and misery she had faced and the anxiety of her immediate future. If she had the nerve to walk out now, to put on her crumpled dress and escape into the night, she had the certain feeling that Blake would stalk her silently until she was secured again. Mary wanted her and what Mary wanted, Mary got. Blake had assured her of that. His affection for her aunt seemed to be his only weakness.

The nightmare returned, more terrifying than ever. The smoke was black, suffocating, a mask of terror to hide the bright, leaping flames. Heat was all around her, penetrating her throat, stopping her breath, and the roaring of the fire, the sound of falling timbers, drowned out her screams. She reached out, trying to get to her father, shouting his name, feeling her senses going as she saw his face.

'*Nicola!*'

Hard, strong hands lifted her, forcing her upwards. Hard arms slid around her, supporting her as her head just fell back.

'*Nicola!*'

The voice filtered through into her dreams, penetrating the world of fear she drifted in and Nicola tried to force her eyes open, her ears picking up the sound of her own moaning, the memory of terrified screams still in her head.

'Daddy! Why?' She called despairingly and Blake shook her none to gently.

'Wake up, Nicola!' he ordered fiercely. 'Come out of it! You're dreaming.' She managed to get her eyes open then, her head still resting lifelessly against the shoulder that now supported her, and she stared at Blake with tear-filled green eyes that barely saw him.

'It's all right,' he insisted sharply. 'It's a dream, nothing.'

'Nothing?' she whispered. 'Nothing?'

She could feel hysteria rising in her throat, tightening her chest and her hands clenched on his white shirt as if the feel of it would keep her safe and awake. The memory of the flames was still in her eyes, but slowly they focused as he watched her steadily.

'Blake?' She looked at him with a puzzled frown, slowly recovering, beginning to pull away from him.

'Who else?' he queried sardonically. 'Scream like that again and I'll be inclined to start screaming myself.'

'It was the—the nightmare...'

'Oh, I know that. I half expected it, but I had no idea it was such a blockbuster.' He looked down at her as she anxiously wriggled to get free. 'You're OK now?'

Nicola nodded, but as she sat upright she started to tremble violently and Blake pulled her into his arms again, tucking her close, his hand beginning to stroke her back soothingly. It was wonderfully calming, pushing away the fear, slowly sending the shadow of the flames to the back of her mind. Nicola relaxed and leaned against him, just letting everything drift away, more peaceful than she had been since the fire.

Her tightly clenched hands relaxed too and she took a deep shuddering breath. It was almost gone, but she still luxuriated in the peace. Somewhere at the back of her mind was a puzzle. How could someone so fierce and dominant make her feel like this? At the moment it didn't matter. It was easier just to stay where she was.

'This is a skill I never knew I had,' Blake murmured in a darkly amused voice and she felt guilty at once, the peace vanishing.

'I'm fine, thank you,' she managed huskily and he drew back to look at her, letting her go as she struggled to sit up by herself.

'You're not fine. You just have an astounding ability to freeze into a shell and make declarations. You wouldn't be fine after that traumatic event if you were a hefty weight-lifter.' He tilted her chin and gazed at her with dark, probing eyes, searching her face slowly. He must have been convinced by what he saw because he let her go and stood. 'Better get up and come next door— break the spell. The English need a tray of tea in a crisis, I believe? I'll order one.'

She was still too dazed to really think and she slid from the bed without much consciousness of his presence. When it came to her that he was still there she made a hasty grab for her robe and he looked with wry amusement at her flushed face.

'Well, it's better than the dress,' he murmured mockingly, 'and it fits perfectly.'

He walked out, leaving the door open and Nicola put on her robe with shaking hands. The nightie certainly did fit, like a glove. The lace curved around her breasts and the silk slid smoothly over her hips, a long slit at each side that showed tantalising glimpses of her slender legs as she moved. With the robe tied tightly round her she still hesitated, but she knew Blake's moods by now. If she lingered he would be back. She followed him into the sitting-room and steeled herself to the fact that any moment now somebody would arrive with tea and intrigued looks.

He was just putting the phone down and he glanced at her keenly as she came in and sat on the very edge of a chair.

'Relax,' he ordered. 'Get right out of it before you go back to bed.'

'I'm keeping you up. I'm sorry,' Nicola said quietly, but he shrugged and sat in a facing chair, his eyes drifting slowly over her.

'I only just got back. Luckily I arrived in time to hear you start that screaming. In any case, a late night never bothers me, I'm a night-owl. If I'm working I never look at the clock. Sometimes it's morning and I've never even noticed the night pass.'

'I I expect you get very deeply into things,' Nicola surmised quickly and he raised one dark brow, looking at her quizzically.

'Oh, you'll have to be smarter than that to change the subject,' he taunted. 'I have few social graces. I only bother to talk about things that interest me and right now it's your nightmare.'

'It's not—not interesting,' Nicola assured him in a low voice, dropping her head to escape from his eyes.

'Maybe you can't hear it. It sure interested me after I came back to earth level.' He stopped speaking and Nicola looked up rather fearfully to be instantly captured by piercing dark eyes. 'One day, you'll have to talk about it,' he said quietly.

'It would take a lifetime,' she whispered, thankful when the knock on the door announced the arrival of her tea. Blake got up to answer, but stopped and glanced down at her as he passed.

'Maybe that's how long Mary will want to keep you,' he murmured.

Nicola thought not. Aunt Mary had never tried to get in touch with her brother in all this time. It was unlikely that she would want a niece she had never seen. This insistence on having her to stay was either duty or curiosity. Whatever it was, Nicola had no intention of staying even for a prolonged visit. She would go now because she needed help and acknowledged it. She also knew that her chances of escaping from Blake were remote.

And she was curious herself. She had no idea what Aunt Mary looked like and somehow it had become important to know. Having lost everything, including some of her identity, she wanted some concrete thing to hang on to. A relative, however abysmal, was real. Everything else, including her past life, seemed to be a bad dream.

Next morning Nicola awoke to the sound of voices in the adjoining sitting-room. It was almost nine o'clock and she felt much better. She made no move to get up. Whoever was in there was obviously talking to Blake and she was not about to burst in and be seen, yet again, in her night attire.

After her particularly bad dream she had slept peacefully and she wondered uneasily if it was because of

Blake. Nobody had held her and comforted her since the fire. She had been in hospital, carefully looked after, but there had been no shoulder to cry on, no arms to hold her. Blake had been the first person to do that and she felt almost at peace this morning.

Last night she had managed to get out of talking, but Blake had been there and it had helped. He had even looked kind, in a hard sort of way. It did not mean that she could let her guard down, and she knew it, but it must show that under the fierce, blazing power there was some sort of gentleness.

She changed her mind almost at once as Blake came to the door and knocked sharply.

'Nicola! Breakfast!' he announced clearly and coldly. 'Get it now. We have plenty to do today. You can shower later. The meal is served.'

She understood then who had been talking—the waiter again, no doubt getting sharp orders. She got out of bed and went to get a quick wash, giving her hair an equally quick comb through. Blake was back to normal: hard as nails and handing out dictatorial instructions. Nicola went through to the sitting-room with a grim look on her face, her gratitude quite gone.

Not that he noticed. A table was already prepared and, as Nicola came in, Blake pulled out a chair for her, sitting then and beginning his own breakfast.

'I waited for you,' he pointed out briskly. 'After this we have several people coming.'

'But—but I'm not ready! I mean, I've only really got this to wear and...'

'That's why they're coming. As you'll have to be changing and trying things on, it seems to me that you're in the ideal garments to start off. Your hair will be done, too,' he finished with a glance at Nicola's thick golden hair that shone in the morning sunlight.

'I'm capable of washing my own hair!' she informed him sharply, and he looked at her as if she was quite mad and definitely of a lower order. No doubt, in his circle, nobody lifted a finger to see to themselves.

'Why should you? In any case, it needs seeing to.'

'Seeing to? This is my hair, on my head! Nobody is cutting it off!'

Her aggressive attitude evidently surprised Blake because he stopped, his coffee-cup halfway to his mouth.

'You mean the hair or the head? I'm beginning to wonder about the head. Right now, though, I didn't have that in mind. The hair needs a trim.'

'Did you start out as a lady's maid before you went into films?' Nicola asked waspishly, taking back every kind thought about him, and she got that worrying tiger grin immediately.

'When I'm with a lady, she usually gives the maid the night off,' he assured her in a deriding voice. 'As to the hair and my knowledge, it's my business to know how people look and how they should look. The hair needs a trim.'

Nicola glared at him and opened her mouth to say more, but his hand shot out and the long, hard fingers curled around her wrist like a steel band.

'Don't give me any trouble, Nicola,' he warned darkly. 'I've picked you up and I'm transporting you to America. That's the promise I made to Mary. The packaging is up to me. Before the day is out, you'll be dressed to suit me and your golden locks will be professionally washed and trimmed.'

'And if I refuse, in front of the hairdresser?' Nicola asked rebelliously, tossing her head and tugging to get her hand free.

'I'll spank you.' His hand slid from her wrist as he made this outrageous statement, but it went no further than her own hand, his fingers holding her fast as his thumb massaged her palm in a sensuous, suggestive manner that brought deep colour racing under her skin.

Nicola stared at him silently, too anxious to make another move. She was suddenly, tremblingly aware that this was not just Blake Anderson, famous, rich and autocratic. This was a devastatingly attractive man. She was staying here alone with him and, at the moment, his masculinity was making her heart race.

Blake watched her in narrow-eyed amusement and then let her go, withdrawing his hand slowly and caressingly, his fingertips trailing over her palm. His smile grew and he sat back to regard her with a satisfied look.

'One thing you learn in my business,' he commented softly, 'is if a line of attack fails, come at it from another angle immediately. I have plenty of angles left in my box of tricks,' he added, never taking his eyes from her.

Nicola took a deep, shuddering breath and made herself sit up straight and face him.

'If you mean that you're quite prepared to manhandle me to get your own way...' she began haughtily, and Blake gave a low laugh that shivered its way down her spine.

'Why, Nicola!' he taunted darkly. 'You're devious. Here am I thinking that you're the perfect English innocent and you're slyly wriggling, quite prepared to ignore the obvious.'

'I'm not going with you!' Nicola declared shakily. 'I want to leave! I'm not safe with you.'

Blake just continued with his breakfast after one sceptical look at her.

'Better reconsider,' he suggested mockingly. 'You're safer with me than you would be if you walked out of here in your nightie. In any case, it was merely a threat to a naughty girl who has a tendency to snap and be defiant.' He shrugged without even looking up at her. 'You could have the spanking instead, or you could travel with me in that peculiar dress you had on when I collected you.' He looked up then and there was no amusement whatever in the dark eyes that stabbed at her from beneath black brows. 'Whatever you decide, though, you're with me as I told you and, as I also told you, the next person you're with—is Mary.'

Nicola subsided and tried to eat. By now she had the feeling that he would get his own way under any circumstances and she had no idea why that should surprise her, he had a reputation for getting his own way. He had made it quite clear that if she walked out of here she would be doing it in either the night attire or the sadly crumpled dress. She didn't have the nerve and she knew it. Her bank was miles away now.

There wasn't much time for thinking. She left the room as soon as she reasonably could and at least escaped another encounter with a waiter. She had just finished showering when the stream of people with clothes began to arrive and Nicola went through one of the most embarrassing times of her life because Blake insisted on seeing everything she tried on, except the undies.

She had to admit that the clothes were beautiful, exactly the things she would have chosen herself if she had ever had so much money and, when it came to it, she couldn't choose at all.

'Anything you don't care for?' Blake asked coolly when the last garment had been tried.

'No. They're all lovely,' Nicola told him quietly and he turned to the assistants who stood like so many breathless slaves, waiting.

'Leave the lot,' he ordered, taking out his chequebook.

Nicola said nothing at all until the last delighted person had left, then she turned to Blake with a look of desperation.

'Did you see the price tags? I can't afford more than one outfit and that would almost empty my account. There are twelve outfits!'

'So?' he enquired harshly. 'You'll need all of them and plenty more. I don't remember asking you to pay for anything at all. The clothes are on me, so is the hair. As to this bank that you're pestering my life with, I'll take you later.' He glanced at his watch and frowned. 'Assuming it's where I found you,' he muttered, reminding Nicola of his tale about the stray cat, 'it's going to be a three-hour round trip.'

'I—I can take a train...' Nicola began, and she got a stony look, the dark brows raised derisively.

'In your nightie? These clothes are for your coming trip to the States. You wear them as we go through that door, *only* if I'm with you.'

'You don't trust me!' Nicola accused angrily, and hard fingers tilted her flushed face.

'Oh, I do!' he mocked. 'I trust you completely—when I have my hands on you. At other times, I wouldn't turn my back or you'd be off like a rocket and I'd have the irritating task of looking for you.'

'You wouldn't even bother!' Nicola retorted hopefully, uselessly attempting to turn her face away.

'Oh, I *would*,' he taunted, the dark eyes capturing her gaze and swallowing her up. 'You see, I'm to deliver you to Mary and I have this reputation to protect. I never lose and I haven't lost a woman yet.'

Nicola's trembling awareness was beginning to make her legs buckle, but she was saved by the arrival of the hairdresser who was ushered in by Blake and sent in the direction of Nicola's bathroom with curt orders.

'Keep the style, it suits her. Just a trim. No more than one centimetre.'

'Your husband knows his own mind,' the hairdresser commented as she closed the bedroom door firmly. Her face was rather red and Nicola could see that Blake had not made a friend there.

'He—he's looking after me,' Nicola soothed anxiously. 'He's my—my cousin.'

'Relatives!' the woman snorted and Nicola nodded in agreement. Fortunately, he wasn't one, neither was he a husband, if he had been she would have run out in her nightie and startled London without a qualm.

They caught the first flight out the next morning and Nicola sat beside Blake and tried to face things calmly. The journey had started and Blake had got his own way, as usual.

She glanced at him secretly and then looked away. He was obviously quite used to jetting all over the world, but she was not. Right from the first she had been obliged to rely on him and now she was completely at his mercy.

They had visited the bank and she had money now, but it was simply a small amount, barely enough to get her back home after this trip. She had never bothered to save. The future had always seemed bright and secure. Now she felt very insecure and sitting there in first class, surrounded by people who were clearly wealthy, accompanied by a man who radiated power and authority, made Nicola more nervous than ever.

'Calm down,' Blake growled, his eyes still on the book he was reading. 'Nothing is about to happen.'

That wasn't true as she knew very well. What was about to happen was that she would meet a woman she didn't know and have to pretend an interest she didn't feel. Blake would probably stand over her to make sure she said all the right things and smiled in the right places.

She suddenly remembered that he had said that Aunt Mary had been injured in an accident. What sort of accident? How had it curtailed her life? She looked across at Blake and, once again, he knew without even glancing at her.

'Let's have it,' he sighed, taking his eyes from his book with obvious reluctance. It made her feel like an irritating child and Nicola flushed uncomfortably.

'I was just remembering that you said Aunt Mary had had an accident and...'

'A riding accident,' he said briefly, going back to his reading. 'She's in a wheelchair.'

That was when panic really hit Nicola. That was when she quite understood why she was being taken so determinedly to America. Her father's sister was an invalid, crippled, and Blake was making sure that Aunt Mary had everything she wanted. What was it all about? Was she going to be pressurised into being a sort of companion? She just couldn't do it and she would not! She had a good brain, a technical brain.

'I won't stay,' she said quietly, fighting hard to control the panic in her voice, and Blake turned slowly to look at her with hard eyes.

'Let's cross that particular bridge when we come to it,' he suggested coldly. 'For the time being, I'm reasonably satisfied with events. I've got the première over and, in spite of a good deal of harassment, I have you here with me, all according to plan. At this moment, you can't walk away. Make your mind up when we get there.'

'So far I haven't had any choice,' Nicola reminded him a trifle bitterly and he turned back to his book with an air of impatience that totally dismissed her.

'Your idea of a choice was ludicrous and you know it,' he bit out. 'A down-market hotel, a cheap dress and work when you felt able.' He shot a glittering glance at her. 'I don't know anything about your upbringing, but I know Mary, and you're her niece. You're used to good things. I only have to look at your face to know you wouldn't survive in a harsh environment.'

'I haven't always looked weak and worn out,' Nicola snapped in a low voice, very conscious of fellow passengers. 'I can hold my own with no difficulty.'

'A tough English rose? Sure,' he surmised scornfully. 'Why is it that I can't imagine it?' He went back to his book and Nicola subsided into silence. It was pointless to argue anyway because, as he had ruthlessly pointed out, she couldn't just walk away now; they were high up over the Atlantic and, at the other side, she would be a stranger in a strange land with nothing of her own but a small amount of cash and a cheque-book with not much backing to it.

She felt more frightened than ever, more at his mercy than ever and the only way to survive the flight was to sleep. She put her seat back and resolutely closed her eyes, irritated beyond words when she heard Blake give a grunt of satisfaction that signified his relief that she was momentarily out of his hair.

Her eyes seemed to have barely closed when the nightmare hit her. She could feel the heat again, see the smoke again and the cruel, curling flames. She tossed in her seat, moaning, fighting the scream that was rising in her throat, but it never actually got there. Her seat was propelled upright and Blake brought her to the present with a tight grip on her shoulders as he turned her to face him, forcing her out of sleep.

'Nicola!' he said warningly and she blinked her eyes, her hands clutching at his arms.

'It—it was...'

'I know,' he assured her quietly. Even just out of her nightmare there was this instinct to hide in whispers, to let no one else know, and she realised that if Blake had not been there she would have been screaming wildly and terrifying the other passengers. Even here, even flying to another land, she was having fearful dreams.

'It's never going to go away,' she whispered despairingly, tears coming to her eyes and beginning to run down her cheeks.

'It is!' Blake insisted sharply. 'You just need time.'

'Time? You think time will heal this? You think I'll forget the terror, the fact that my father died?'

Tears were streaming down her face, her cheeks were wet and Blake's eyes narrowed ominously, his hands still gripping her fiercely.

'Don't tell me again about shooting off back to England,' he warned darkly. 'Forget the escape routine. Who the hell was going to help you if I hadn't arrived? Where were your friends, your buddies, your long line of male admirers? That doctor at the hospital told me you had nobody. Well, now, you've got somebody. You've got Mary—and you've got me!'

'I don't know her,' Nicola insisted, trying to stifle the tears, unable even to wipe them away because she was being held too tightly to get free. 'I'll just be a stranger.'

'You didn't know me,' Blake reminded her, 'but we've shared an hotel suite. I've rescued you from two nightmares and you know me now. It didn't take long.'

'I don't know you,' Nicola protested in a choked voice, shaking her head and licking at her tears frantically. 'I don't want to know you. You're right out of my world and—and you're almost frightening.'

'I'm real!' he stated harshly, his voice still low and hard. 'I don't lurk in your dreams. If I frighten you, you can lash out at me and, as you seem inclined to do just that, I can't be too frightening.'

It was true and Nicola was looking at him with a puzzled expression on her face when the stewardess began to serve drinks. She was almost level with them. They had been so wrapped up in their conversation that neither of them had noticed her and now Nicola struggled, her wet cheeks flooding with embarrassed colour.

'She'll see,' she began in an agitated voice. 'She'll know I've been crying.'

'What does it matter?' Blake looked at her angrily as she pulled free and searched for her handkerchief, hurriedly trying to get the signs of misery off her face.

'It matters to me. I'm enough of a freak as it is, having to be rescued, having to be looked after... I don't want anyone to know that I'm not normal.'

'That's soon remedied,' Blake muttered, reaching for her and pulling her into his arms, 'although I'm inclined to agree that you're anything but normal.'

Nicola had no time to react and the problem of anyone seeing her tears was solved with no difficulty. She was wrapped securely in Blake's arms in an instant and his mouth covered hers so swiftly and firmly that she had no time to even gasp for breath.

The outrage she should have felt never materialised. His lips were insistent, dominating and he was not merely pretending to kiss her. It was all real and Nicola raised trembling hands to ward him off, her fear of the stewardess seeing her distress now quite gone. Nothing was in her mind but the thought of escaping because Blake was kissing her so thoroughly that her bones were beginning to feel as if they were melting.

Sensations she had never felt before began to race through her and Nicola pushed at his hard chest, knowing she must escape at any cost. She could feel her breasts swelling, the nipples tight and pained. It had never happened to her before and it embarrassed her, her anxiety that he should discover this shame making her struggle still. Heat seemed to be growing inside her from some deep source, but Blake had no intention of allowing her to escape. His hand moved to cup her face, his thumb trailing slowly along her jawline and, with his other arm tightly around her, she was a prisoner.

A terrible excitement was spreading through her body and she was losing any will to resist at all. Nicola knew it but there was nothing she could do. Her lips were softening, parting, as his mouth moved over hers and the hands that had pushed so feverishly against him now clutched his shirt. Slowly her head began to fall back as a sensuous relaxation flooded through her limbs. She became pliant, intoxicated by the movement of his lips, her breathing slowing to a deep, steady rhythm.

Her senses were swimming and she just gazed up at him with dazed eyes when Blake lifted his head. For a moment she had no idea where she was and she looked back into the dark, narrowed eyes with no thought of either looking away or protesting. For a few moments she had been in an enchanted world.

'Another crisis over,' Blake murmured, his eyes travelling slowly over her face. 'She never took our orders.'

Nicola just lay against his arm, her body still throbbing with unaccustomed feeling, her mind trying to reassert itself. He had controlled her so very quickly, obliterated her own personality with skilful ease. Had her shocking experience in the fire and the aftermath of that left her defenceless? Why wasn't she protesting now? At any other time she would have sat back and hit him, but she was still lying there, her lips throbbing from his kiss, her eyes unwillingly drawn to his hard, firm mouth.

Blake's hand slowly moved from her face, his fingers trailing over her flushed skin and then he moved away, leaving her, glancing round to find the stewardess, and Nicola took a steadying breath. She knew she had to say something, do something, but she could not even think at the moment. She just blurted out her feelings with no thought behind the words at all.

'Why did you kiss me like that?'

'Like what?' he asked vaguely. He never looked at her—he was still busy trying to catch the stewardess's eye—more interested in ordering a drink than the fact that he had reduced Nicola to a shivering person whose legs wouldn't move and whose blood seemed to have become too thick and hot to move easily in her veins.

'You *know* how!' she managed in a low, uneven voice.

'But I do it all the time.' He turned to look at her wryly. 'I often have to give a lesson for the benefit of my leading man. It has to look right on film. It's second nature.'

It was worse than ever then, utterly humiliating, and Nicola turned her face away abruptly, looking out of the window although there was nothing to see but white, feathery clouds. A lesson in acting and she had been swept under like a storm-tossed boat with the ocean thundering over it. Blake had felt nothing but a need to be technically accurate, and she had been mindless.

CHAPTER FOUR

NICOLA felt rage growing deep inside and she didn't much care if it was a self-protecting mechanism to smother her humiliation. The stewardess came and smiled down at Blake in admiration, a look in her eyes that had Nicola turning back to her furious contemplation of the clouds.

'Drinks, Mr Anderson?' It was a sexy voice, Nicola decided, and Blake played up to it willingly.

'Two brandies, I think,' he drawled with a quizzical smile. 'We missed you first time round.'

'I noticed.' The stewardess gave him another knowing look and left, and Nicola turned on him furiously.

'I can see that you're as well known in the air as you are on the ground,' she seethed. 'She had no trouble with your name.'

'Why should she?' Blake asked in a reasonable voice 'In first class she probably has every name at her fingertips.'

'I bet she doesn't know my name,' Nicola hissed, glaring into his amused face. 'Being with you is an embarrassment. It's like travelling with Father Christmas in full dress uniform! Who could miss you?'

'When you're quite well, you'll be a handful,' Blake surmised slowly, reaching out to tilt her face. She snatched it away and he gave a low laugh. 'I can't help it if people know me. You want me to wear a mask?'

'Quite pointless!' Nicola snapped. 'It wouldn't hide your ego!'

The drinks arrived while Blake was still laughing and Nicola took hers with very bad grace, especially as the look in the eyes of the stewardess said quite clearly, What a lucky girl you are.

'OK,' Blake murmured when they were back to a peculiar sort of privacy. 'Next time you have a bad dream, I'll just shake you.'

'I was awake!' Nicola pointed out furiously.

'But you were in a panic. You were wanting a place to hide,' he reminded her softly. 'I hid you.'

Which was perfectly true if you had an odd way of looking at things, Nicola mused crossly. He had hidden her tear-stained face from interested eyes and he had brought her a lot of unwanted attention too. The couple across the aisle were amused and intrigued, and now she hardly dared sit forward. She had uneasy thoughts of the incident being passed along in whispers and she drank her drink almost straight off, to Blake's obvious amusement.

'You want another, Nicola?' he asked with mocking concern and she absolutely refused to answer. He went back to his book and, when Nicola glanced at him in annoyance, he was reading avidly. But he had that nasty tiger grin back on his face so she picked up her magazine and ignored him as much as she could.

It was not at all easy. She was still in a turmoil inside and she hoped he didn't realise that. Anger had not driven away the ecstatic feelings that he had brought to her body. Even her heart was not back to normal. No wonder he got exactly what he was after on film if he gave demonstrations of that sort of thing. Starry-eyed heroines would be very easy to produce for the camera. The leading man would have nothing to do.

Nicola chewed anxiously at her lip and wondered uneasily how things would have been if they had not been trapped in an aircraft with so many interested onlookers. Surviving would not have been easy and she had to pull herself up very sharply as she began to think about it. Blake had merely been playing a part he had played often enough before. It would not have been necessary to survive. He would have drawn back and smiled that superior smile.

Pity his girlfriends! They would never know when he was acting or being serious. His path to fame must have been strewn with broken hearts. It was odd that she had never thought of that aspect of things when she had been contemplating his arrogant bearing and his ruthless ability to get his own way. But why should she have thought of it? She had never expected to be a victim.

It put a different light on his kindness the other night, too, when he had held her and comforted her. More acting—and she had been grateful! At that moment she was filled with seething rage. In spite of her body's un-accustomed feelings, anger was almost choking her. It would be absolutely wonderful to be fending off this monster while Aunt Mary was trying to get her to stay and play nursemaid!

The flight seemed endless and Nicola was exhausted. She had not dared to sleep again in case the nightmare caused her any more problems. Every time she felt her eyes getting heavy, she shot up in her seat and made herself stay awake. The in-flight film helped to pass a little of the time, but mostly it was tedious.

'You can sleep,' Blake said quietly, glancing across at her. 'I'll keep an eye on you.'

But Nicola shook her head, avoiding his eyes. She had still not recovered completely from the aftermath of her last attempt at sleep and now she was uneasy with him, terribly aware that he was close beside her. There was a tingling in the air between them that had not been there before.

He was travelling in casual clothes like many of the Americans on the flight. It was easy to spot them, there was something relaxed and self-assured about them, but even in this atmosphere, Blake was different. His hard, handsome features were filled with forceful character and she assumed that he was like that because of his way of life. Vulnerability was not something easy to imagine with Blake.

She glanced at him secretly, her eyes drawn to the way his lean, athletic body fitted snugly inside his clothes. He wore a dark blue sports shirt, the neck open and showing the tanned column of his throat. He was superbly masculine in every way possible and Nicola hastily looked away as her eyes roamed to the way his strong thighs stretched the material of the dark trousers he wore. She had a sudden flare of panic as she imagined the strength of his legs against hers, his hard arms around her.

It was madness! She blushed and inspected her own hands minutely, trying to ease the strain of her suddenly tight breathing. Blake was still reading. As far as she had been able to tell, he had finished the book and started it all over again. Even so, he seemed to be absorbed. At the moment she was very glad about that.

She glanced at his face, keeping her eyes strictly from his body. A thick lock of dark hair had fallen across his forehead and he pushed it away with a careless hand. He had beautiful hands, long-fingered and strong, tanned deeply gold as the rest of him was tanned.

Nicola looked away again very rapidly, swallowing hard as deep colour flooded to the surface of her skin. She had no idea what the rest of him was like, she had seen nothing but his face and neck, but she was conjecturing like a lunatic! She had never even thought about the male body before and now she was wading deeper into problems, on the edge of indulging in strictly forbidden fantasies. All because of one kiss and a deceptive kiss at that, a great piece of acting on the spur of the moment.

'Careful. I bite.' Blake's dark, derisive voice warned her that he was well aware of her scrutiny and Nicola had to do some fast thinking.

'I was wondering why you live so far away from Los Angeles,' she said quickly, congratulating herself on this speedy innovation when her heart was racing with fright.

'Were you?' He glanced at her ironically, his eyes skimming slowly over her flushed cheeks. 'Did you have to work out how much I weighed before you asked, in case I objected to the question and decided to beat you?'

Nicola's face simply flooded with more colour at this intimation that he had not only observed her scrutiny, but also had been aware of her lingering glances at his body.

'I thought you might be too—too involved with your book to want to speak,' she managed breathlessly. 'It was just an idle thought. I wondered why you didn't live in Hollywood or somewhere near.'

'Somewhere near what?' he enquired wryly, watching her with amused eyes. 'Nowadays, most films are made on location, or, at least, the main part of them. Living next to a studio is not necessary. In any case, I usually choose my own locations. I live where I want to live and I go where it's at!'

'That's a very American way of speaking,' Nicola observed, glad for an excuse to be prim after her disgraceful speculations, and he shot her a glance of ironic astonishment.

'I *am* American! What do you expect?'

'I'm sorry,' Nicola muttered, looking back at her hands and escaping from the derisive eyes. 'I suppose you think I'm impertinent?'

'Impertinent?' he queried leisurely, rolling the word round to savour it. 'No, I don't think you're impertinent. I think you're odd. It's entertaining—in small doses.'

He went straight back to his book and Nicola sat very still, struggling with mixed feelings. There was an urgent need to shout at him, even to hit him, but there was an even more urgent need to control the renewed trembling that had come just because he had looked at her closely.

Somehow he had managed to set up a storm inside her and it was purely sexual. Without any experience of it before, she still recognised the feeling and it scared and embarrassed her. One superbly technical kiss and he had achieved this! She would have to make sure he never suspected or he would think her more than odd, and she just couldn't stand his sarcasm. In any case, the feeling would soon go.

She took a slow, steady breath, trying to return to normal, making herself relax.

'Ask anything else you like when you have another idle thought,' Blake said silkily, his eyes on his book. 'There's no need to assess my physical capabilities. I never hit women.'

Nicola dived into her magazine. So far she had read it from cover to cover, but now she started again. If Blake could read something twice right off, then so could she. And he knew exactly how she was feeling. He had probably stood back and grinned that tiger grin when he had brought this feeling to some unsuspecting actress. It was all deceit, despicable!

'You're tired.' Blake made this flat statement when they were speeding down the highway on the last leg of their journey. He had picked up his car when they landed and at least there was no possibility of strangers observing if she decided to make a fool of herself again. Nicola stopped the thought at once. What was Blake but a stranger? He was a very dangerous stranger, too, and her recent attitude was making him more dangerous still.

'I thought the journey would never end,' she said, weariness in her voice that could not be hidden. 'I'm quite surprised that it tired me so much.'

'However comfortably you travel, flying is always tiring. In your case, too exhausting for words, I would think. You probably needed another couple of weeks before tackling that flight.'

When she glanced across at him he was frowning darkly, his eyes narrowed on the sunlit road.

'Well, you made me come,' she reminded him, and he shot her a sideways glance that was almost sinister.

'I had to collect you. I did not have time to wait for your complete recovery. You'll recover here.' His eyes went back to the road and Nicola felt she had just escaped a strike of lightning. Any mention of her not going on with him and his temper rose without warning. She suddenly had the feeling that she would find it very difficult to get away and return to England. Her main hope seemed to lie in the possibility that Aunt Mary would not like her. In such a case she had not the slightest doubt that Blake would dispatch her with the same sort of ruthlessness he had shown in capturing her.

It was a beautiful road and, if she had not been so weary, Nicola would have been sitting up straight and taking a lot of notice. Even in her present state she was quite enchanted, and her eyes skimmed from side to side of the car as she tried to see everything at once.

It seemed in places to have been carved from the mountains, the Pacific Ocean, sun-tossed and inviting at the other side. Sometimes they were skirting the ocean, sometimes darting inland to pass through small towns with a distinct Spanish flavour, but always the road ran on like a ribbon carefully placed among beauty.

'It's lovely,' Nicola breathed and Blake shot a look at her that turned to amusement when he saw her entranced face.

'State Highway number one,' he informed her. 'The Wonderful One.'

'That's what you call it?' Nicola asked in surprise and she got that dark amusement again.

'Not me, no,' he told her drily. 'I'm not much given to offering compliments to roads. I was telling you its title. That's what it's called. It runs for a very long way. You get a sort of kaleidoscope of California along this road.'

'I'd love to travel along the road and see everything,' Nicola breathed dreamily, her mind taken up with the startling beauty of the mountains and the small inviting coves washed by the ocean.

'One day, if you're very good,' Blake promised mockingly, 'I'll take you.'

'I was thinking of going alone!' Nicola assured him in a sharp voice. She had heard the scathing irony, as if she was a demented patient escaped from observation. Her cheeks flushed angrily and Blake's soft laughter did nothing to make her feel easier in her mind.

'What do you drive, a bike?' he drawled and she absolutely refused to answer. Of course he wouldn't have bothered to find out that she was extremely well qualified at her job. He probably thought she had sat at home doing delicate embroidery. Her temper was simmering, almost ready to boil, and she decided that silence was a good idea. She was at his mercy—temporarily!

Nicola had no idea how long she slept, but the sudden opening of the door at her side made her open her eyes. Blake was standing looking down at her, his expression enigmatic. For a moment she just looked back, not quite sure of where she was. There was an odd feeling in the air, a dream-like feeling. They stared at each other, his dark eyes probing relentlessly and she suddenly came to her senses and moved.

'I must have slept,' she murmured. She felt confused, unable to go on meeting the dark, glittering eyes that watched her so steadily.

'For a long time,' Blake agreed. 'You'll be pleased to know that we've arrived, at last.'

Nicola wasn't pleased. A shiver ran over her skin and it was nothing to do with the atmosphere outside the car. She was very anxious, almost afraid. Blake's hard, handsome features seemed more ruthless than ever at this moment and she hoped it was just her state of disorientation after a sleep. She got out of the car and he moved back to allow her to stand freely. He didn't move very far though, as if he expected her to just collapse and, as she stood, she found herself uneasily close to the hard wall of his chest.

It was a relief to feel the sun on her skin. It was somehow reassuring, normal and Nicola looked around with wide eyes. Her last memory of the journey had been the lovely road, the spectacular scenery, but now she actually caught her breath.

They were parked beside a house that seemed to have come from some film set. It was white, very splendid, the curved front facing the sea. There were porticos fronting the huge door, tall pillars that stood like sentries and looked across the glitter of a blue bay. She could see windows open to the air, white silk curtains blowing softly in the breeze, and they must have come along some great private drive while she slept because there was no sign of any other dwelling—the house obviously stood in extensive grounds.

From here she had no idea how big the house was, but she could see that there was some sort of extension on one side and, as well as that, the building stretched a long way back. The side facing the sea, though, was enough to keep her still and silent for a good while, and then Nicola turned and looked at the view there would be from those huge windows.

Lawns stretched to the edge of a cliff and she could see, as the cliff curved away, that it was made of rocks that tumbled headlong to the sea. Everywhere there were flowers and, spectacularly, great clusters of Marguerite chrysanthemums and tiny geraniums, massed on the rocky edge of the lawn and cascading down the cliff, their bright flowers like small stars fallen from a blue sky.

'Oh!' No other words would come out. Nicola had never seen anything so beautiful as this place, not even her own lovely home that was now reduced to melancholy ruins. She just stood and stared, barely conscious at this moment of the close proximity of Blake's lean, powerful body.

'Do you mean, oh, what a surprise, or is your exclamation part of that strange English saying—oh, my goodness?'

'Please don't spoil it. I've never seen anywhere as beautiful,' Nicola said, her voice almost a whisper.

'Better than staying in a small, cheap hotel within walking distance of the bank?' he asked drily, and Nicola turned on him at once, the dreamy look dying from her eyes.

'That was only going to be a temporary arrangement,' she said sharply. 'This is only a temporary arrangement, too.'

'We'll see,' Blake murmured infuriatingly as he watched her steadily.

'We will not see!' Nicola insisted, standing her ground. 'If you have any unscrupulous thoughts sliding round in your head, then I'm staying right here and not moving.'

'OK,' he muttered unconcernedly, locking the car and turning away. 'It will be dark eventually and it can get chilly at night, especially if you're standing still. Round about ten, I'll come out and throw a blanket over you, then I'll get back to my unscrupulous thoughts.'

He just set off towards the house and Nicola stood dumbfounded. Now that he had her here, he was quite capable of leaving her standing by herself for hours, she just knew it.

'Mr Anderson!' She called to him in a brisk and irritated voice, but he never even turned his head and Nicola could see that she was going to look extremely foolish after a while, staying out here and refusing to go in and meet her aunt.

'Blake!' There was a slight quiver of panic in her voice this time and Blake turned and looked at her, his tiger grin back in place.

'So you remembered my name?' he enquired softly. 'Don't forget it again, because that's what you call me.' He walked slowly back towards her and stood looking down into her eyes. Nicola just stared back and his hand came to cup her face and tilt it up even further. 'Never make threats that you're not prepared to see through to the end,' he warned. 'In the first place, I don't scare at all. In the second place, I'm much too good at threatening to be worried by amateurs. I carry out my threats.'

'You—you mean you would have left me here? You would have left me here all night?'

'With a blanket round you,' he mocked in an aggrieved voice. 'I don't remember ever being actually cruel.' He suddenly laughed, a short, low laugh that worried her and, before she could recover from her slight attack of shock, he took her arm and turned her to the house. 'Come on,' he urged. 'I'd better present you to Mary before your green eyes swallow up your face. I think you're going to take a good deal of looking after,' he ended in a deep murmur.

'I can take care of myself,' Nicola snapped.

'Time will tell, my dear Nicola,' he said sardonically. 'For now, though, you look as if you should be in bed.'

'You're always mentioning bed,' Nicola complained crossly. 'Almost every time you've seen me you've been trying to get me to go to bed.'

Blake stopped and turned to look at her, his eyes moving suggestively over her angry face.

'Have I? If you impart that information to Mary,' he warned softly, 'please don't put it quite like that. Mary has faith in me.'

It was only then that Nicola realised how she had phrased her complaint and her cheeks flushed rose-red and she looked away quickly. His softly sardonic voice also added to her confusion and when she saw a small man in a white jacket emerge from the house, a wide smile on his dark face, she was more than glad to see someone else, even if it was a complete stranger.

'The luggage, Señor Anderson?' The man looked Mexican and Blake grinned at him, tossing him the car keys.

'Thanks, Pablo. Mrs Anderson in her quarters?'

'She is, *señor*. She is excited.'

'Aren't we all?' Blake murmured drily as he took Nicola's arm in an even more firm grip, fearing, apparently, that she would take to her heels and go back to her stubborn stance by the car.

She had pricked up her ears at his remark about Aunt Mary, too. In her quarters? It was unexpected and not a little chilling. This was Blake's house, as he had told her. Was Aunt Mary confined to just one part of it? Was she so much of an invalid? Or did Blake keep her safely stashed away in case she escaped? It seemed more than likely that escape was something she would finally have to think about herself.

'I'll take you to see Mary first,' Blake said briskly, his seductive irony fading away as if it had never been. 'You'll be wanting to freshen up, no doubt, but Mary has been waiting and she can't climb stairs to burst in on you eagerly.'

'That's all right,' Nicola said in a suitably dignified voice. 'Naturally, I want to see her, too.'

'Naturally?' Blake drawled. 'Since when has that entered your attitude? It seems to me, Nicola, that you've been wanting to escape ever since I came for you.'

She noted that word 'escape' and assumed that Blake had thought of her final departure too. She had to get the upper-hand with him if she was to survive this trip.

'Aunt Mary is the only relative I have,' she pointed out in a prickly voice. 'Even if she were not, it's only courtesy to meet her at once.'

'Well, I can be assured of your courtesy,' Blake muttered. 'It's the only thing I'm certain of right now. For the rest—we'll see.'

There was a rather menacing tone to his voice and, when Nicola glanced at him apprehensively, his face had taken on a grim look that did not bode well for the rest of the day.

They walked into a huge hall where a great curving staircase swept up to the upper storeys of the house. Everything seemed to be white and shining, the sunlight glittering off the gleaming handles of the doors that ranged around the hall and Blake led her into a very large room that overlooked the sea.

Even if she had not been able to hear the ocean and see the white-topped waves, Nicola would have known that this room was at the front of the house because the wall on the seaward side was curved as the house had been when she had first looked at it. It made for a very unusual room and, once again, there was an air of wealth and comfort that she had never quite encountered before.

It had the look of some of the wonderful houses she had seen on film and, as her feet sank into thick, pale carpet, Nicola was very impressed. From the pictures on the walls to the glow of the carefully preserved, antique furniture, it was perfect.

'Did you design this room yourself?' she asked in a rather awe-stricken voice.

'I did not. I have more to do with my time,' Blake growled. 'I don't design the sets, if you think that's what it looks like.'

'I think it's beautiful,' Nicola said huffily, annoyed that she had ventured into ordinary conversation and, yet again, had been put down smartly.

'I'll pass on your compliments. For myself, I prefer something more primitive. I have a cabin further up the coast. When I'm knee-deep in work, that's where I go.'

Nicola couldn't help feeling relief. It meant that he would not be around all the time. For one thing, he probably had a film on the go and, for another, thinking back to that book and the time he had spent reading it so avidly, he would most likely take himself off to work at the cabin very soon. Maybe the book was for a new film?

His departure couldn't be soon enough for her because Blake was a danger and she recognised it. She was much too aware of him in a physical sense, like a young girl overwhelmed by her first sight of a man. Nobody had ever had such an effect on her and she found her eyes running over him in a rather disgraceful way as he walked ahead of her to open the door at the side of the room. Even the way he walked brought a tingle to her skin. It was like following a lithe, prowling cat—a man-eater, and the feelings that kept surging inside her were utterly shameful.

'This is where Mary spends a lot of her time.' Blake turned as he spoke, catching her off-guard and seeing the look on her face. Their eyes met and sparks seemed to fly between them, hanging in the air like electricity. For a second he paused as if he had forgotten what he had been about to say. His eyes were locked with hers, his face suddenly taut, and then he threw open the door and motioned her into another part of the house.

'She never goes upstairs now,' he continued, not looking at Nicola. She used the time to settle her frantic heartbeats and compose her flushed face. This was ridiculous. She had no idea what was happening to her. 'I wanted to have a lift fitted, but she prefers to be here,' Blake murmured. 'She's more capable of things when they're all on one level and she can get out into the garden and generally manage well enough.'

'Does she have a nurse?' Nicola asked, trying to be normal and worriedly wondering when he was going to tell her that she would do as a nurse.

'Pablo's wife, Dolores, looks after Mary,' Blake told her flatly. 'His sister Angelica helps him run the house, so, you see, we're quite a tight-knit unit.'

'Aren't you worried about letting a stranger into the smoothly running arrangement?' Nicola persisted, probing for information that she was sure she would be better off not knowing.

'Are you speaking about yourself, Nicola?' Blake enquired in a voice that seemed to be verging on anger. 'You're no stranger. I know you quite well, and what I don't know I can make a very good guess about. You're not really going to be the wild card in the pack.'

'Because you'll keep me in my place,' Nicola surmised gloomily.

'When I decide what your place is.' He stopped suddenly and tilted her rather glum face up to the light.

'Cheer up, or Mary will think I forced you here unwillingly.'

'You did,' Nicola muttered and he began to laugh, a dark derisive sound that did nothing to fill her with confidence.

'But we don't want her to know that, do we? You and I have secrets that we'll keep from Mary. Her life has to be tranquil and I don't want her to know that you look at me with grave suspicion or that you scream in the night.'

'It's cruel to say that...' Nicola began, but he looked down at her with taunting eyes.

'I'm not cruel. When you need me, don't I come running? I'll keep on doing it so don't lock your door.'

'You said you work in a cabin,' Nicola reminded him quickly as her heart tried to leap into her throat.

'Only when I'm sure you're safe to leave,' he murmured, ushering her in front of him. And that could mean almost anything, Nicola concluded. It could mean that he would keep an eye on her behaviour so that Mary would never be upset. On the other hand he might imagine that she would flee if left unsupervised. She might well give some serious thought to that last idea if he stayed around for very long. She was dreading meeting her aunt, but surely nobody could worry her as much as Blake did? Her problems with him seemed to be growing and some of them were of her own making.

She almost cried with relief when she saw Mary Anderson. It was like seeing her father again, but the quiet face that looked at her eagerly as she walked into the room was much softer, much more gentle than her father's face had been. Aunt Mary showed on the outside what her father had been inside and Nicola wanted to run to her and give her a hug.

She was much too shy, though, much too wary, and with Blake looking on with very alert eyes she tried to compose herself and act normally. She didn't want him thinking she was a near-hysterical wreck. Besides, Aunt Mary was a stranger even though there was this devastating likeness to her father. She was in a wheelchair, a mechanised one, and she swung it round to face them.

Mary Anderson was still a very pretty woman even though there was suffering on her face. She didn't look in any way weak, however. The only sign of any disability was the utter stillness of her legs, lifeless in the silk trousers she wore that matched the brilliantly blue blouse. She wore a lot of jewellery and Nicola gave her full marks for that. Aunt Mary cared about her appearance still, and didn't look the sort of woman who would give up easily.

'Nicola, my dear!' There was the soft whirring of the engine of the chair as Mary came forward to greet the niece she had never seen before, and Nicola came to life belatedly and went to meet her. There were tears in Mary's eyes and Nicola threw caution to the winds and bent to hug her aunt, a strange feeling of happiness flooding through her that she had someone of her own, someone with whom she could show emotion.

She felt tears pricking at the back of her own eyes, but she held them off. There was no way that this meeting would be marred by any sort of upset. For a moment she had forgotten Blake but, as she stood, Mary still clinging to her hand, he came forward, too, bending to kiss his stepmother's cheek.

'Blake, you brought her. I didn't really think you'd manage it.'

'And I thought you had faith in me,' Blake teased, his choice of words reminding Nicola of the warning he had given in his sardonic voice when she had made her rather unfortunate complaint a little while earlier. 'It was no problem,' he continued. 'Nicola and I got on very well indeed. She's a member of the family already.'

'Oh, I do hope so,' Mary said eagerly, smiling up at Nicola.

'She's worn out,' Blake mentioned, with a glance at Nicola's white face. 'Why don't I show her to her room for now? She'll want to freshen up at the very least. You can gossip and get to know each other later.'

'Of course. There's plenty of time,' Mary said happily, patting Nicola's hand, and once again Blake took over in his powerful way.

'All the time in the world,' he murmured, turning Nicola to the door. She said nothing. For one thing, she was no longer filled with dread, and for another she was still too close to tears to start any battle with Blake. She was not now so anxious to escape because she wanted to get to know her aunt. She would be quite content to stay here for a good while, providing that Blake went off to his cabin or disappeared to some film location.

CHAPTER FIVE

'PABLO will have delivered your luggage by now,' Blake informed her, leading her back to the magnificent hall and the great, sweeping staircase. 'I'll just show you your room and then leave you to it.'

He never said a word about his stepmother and Nicola bit her lip, worrying what he would say later, what rules he would lay down, because she couldn't believe he would simply deliver her here and then let things take their course. Blake Anderson arranged things to his own liking and no doubt he would give her instructions as soon as he thought fit. She didn't want any trouble, but she would not bow to his demands at all unless she thought them reasonable.

'Here we are.' He opened a door, once again at the front of the house and Nicola gasped with surprise. It was another huge room—a bedroom at one end and a sitting-room at the other—the only division, a small flight of shallow steps. It was beautiful, too, as the other rooms she had seen had been beautiful and there were French windows opening on to a small balcony that looked out at the sea.

'This was my parents' room,' Blake said quietly, his eyes roaming round speculatively.

'Then I shouldn't be here.' Nicola turned to him with a feeling of agitation and he looked at her levelly.

'Why not? It was a long time ago. When my mother died we moved away from here, although Dad kept the house. It wasn't like this then. When Dad married Mary we lived a good way down the coast. I moved back here

77

later, insisted on buying the house from him and had it all re-designed. The room was not at all like this when they slept in it, so don't worry. You're not intruding.'

'I—I would have thought you'd want this room for yourself,' Nicola ventured in a hesitant voice, and he suddenly smiled, his rather taut expression easing.

'Too feminine for me. My room is opposite, right across the passage.'

'Oh!' Nicola's face flushed for no good reason and she felt a fool at her sudden confusion.

'What was that supposed to mean?' Blake asked in a taunting voice. 'I would have thought you'd be grateful. One scream and I'll hear you. Nobody else will. Mary's too far away and the servants have their own quarters in the grounds.'

'You—you mean we'll be alone in this part of the house?' Nicola asked, her expression alarmed. 'Just you and I?'

'We were alone in the hotel,' he pointed out in amusement. 'I never attacked you. At least, if I did, it's slipped my mind.'

'It just seems—improper.' Nicola didn't know where to look. She had apparently talked herself into a corner and Blake seemed to be appreciating the fact.

'Didn't somebody once say that impropriety is in the mind?' His softly ironic enquiry brought back forcefully the way she had felt on the plane and the fact that he had seemed to know. She turned away, walking on to the balcony and looking out at the sea.

It was so very beautiful, at the moment, calm and safe. Perhaps it wasn't always so. Just like Blake it would be unpredictable.

'Take care if you come out here,' he said, walking out to stand beside her. 'It's a long drop.'

'I'm not thinking of leaping off,' she retorted, willingly going on to the attack to ease her confused thoughts.

'Maybe you'll consider climbing down,' he muttered impatiently. 'Mary may be taken in by your loving greeting, but I've seen your reluctance to come here at first hand.'

'I'm glad I came,' Nicola said, walking back into the room and beginning to open her suitcases, hoping that the action would remind him to leave. 'I won't be troubling you with pleas to send me back to England. I want to get to know Aunt Mary.'

'Why?' He was beside her in two strides, suspicion in his voice. 'You didn't seem too keen before.'

'She looks quite a lot like my father. It—it's a sort of comfort.' Even as she said it, Nicola realised with some surprise that, at this moment, she wouldn't be confessing that to anyone but Blake. It was stupid to confess it to him, too, and she regretted it almost at once.

'You've got to get better without props of that sort,' he said tightly. 'Being here and clinging on to Mary will not get you over the trauma of that night. Only living will do that.'

'I am living!' Nicola snapped, hurt and angry. What did he know about it anyway? 'I didn't have a lot of choice. He saved me and now he's dead.'

'Don't be morbid!' Blake grasped her shoulders and made her face him. He glared at her and Nicola just looked back at him with the old bitterness on her face.

'You're judging without evidence,' she said tightly. 'You don't know the whole story. Even if you did, I don't suppose you'd be different. From the height of your towering importance it must be hard to see the ground.'

Her words made him angry, she could see that and, for a second, he jerked her forward until she was pressed against the unyielding strength of his chest. It didn't make any difference, though. Nicola just looked back at him and he suddenly let her go, turning to the door with that same air of savage impatience about him.

'Come down when you're ready,' he grated. 'I'll be about somewhere. In any case, you know where Mary is.' He didn't slam the door, but it was almost that and Nicola sighed, sinking to the soft bed and staring round at the strange room. Lovely it might be, but it was not her room. She was a stranger in a strange land, everything she owned provided by a man who had taken it upon himself to rearrange her life.

She kicked off her shoes and lay back on the bed for a second and then slowly stretched out. She was so tired. In a minute she would get changed and go down to her aunt. If possible, she would keep out of Blake's way. Her eyes closed and, within seconds, Nicola was fast asleep.

She awoke with a start much later to find a dark face bending over her, gentle hands shaking her. For a second she had no idea where she was and she gasped in alarm.

'It is Dolores, Señorita Rogers. You have slept for a long time and Señor Anderson thought you might like to get ready for dinner now. No hurry. You have almost one hour.'

'Thank you,' Nicola murmured vaguely, her mind beginning to shake off dreams. 'I never meant to go to sleep.' What would they think of her? She had not even been down to speak to her aunt. Blake would be furious.

'The *señor* said you had been ill,' Dolores assured her sympathetically. 'To sleep is good. Señora Anderson sent you a hairdrier, in case you need it, and I have brought you some tea.'

She looked very pleased with herself and Nicola smiled, sitting up on the bed and taking the tea. The sleep had not done her any good at all. It had been deep, filled with anxious dreams and the slight confidence she had been feeling for the past day or two had faded away. She felt unhappy, trapped and lonely, terribly anxious about her immediate future in this household.

Even as she had been coming awake, she had feared Blake's wrath at her discourteous way of behaving. She should have been down to see her aunt and her first coherent thoughts had been that he would reprimand her. She could not go on living like that. She refused to do so.

As she showered and changed for dinner the heavy sadness still would not go and it was hard to bring any sort of pleasant expression to her face as she went down the great sweeping staircase to the rooms below.

She was wearing one of the lovely dresses that Blake had bought for her, glad that the evening air was still warm enough to make a silk dress a possibility. Of course, she could see now why Blake had thought it necessary to buy such expensive garments. It was apparent that nothing but the best would be suitable in these splendid surroundings.

In any case, Blake was accustomed to being with film stars. He would think her very insignificant in the order of things and he had made that quite clear several times. The thought added a further veil of gloom to her mind and she walked into the first room she came to, hearing voices and assuming that they were there.

They were. Aunt Mary obviously did not stay permanently in her own quarters because she was with Blake, having pre-dinner drinks. She turned her chair as Nicola walked in and it was with some relief that Nicola saw a welcoming smile on her aunt's face.

'My dear! I've just been hearing that Blake summoned you to dinner. It would have been perfectly all right to have a meal in your room if you feel unwell.' Her aunt came forward and reached out her hands and

Nicola was only too willing to take them in both of her own. Blake looked cold and dark, no sign of a welcoming smile on his face at all.

He was inspecting her dispassionately, his eyes running over her slowly as if she were dressed for a part and he were checking her suitability. As her eyes met his, he looked at her levelly, no expression at all on that cool, handsome face.

'I'm all right, really,' Nicola told her aunt, tearing her eyes from Blake and the hypnotic effect he had on her. 'I'm sorry I went to sleep. I never intended to. I have no idea how it happened.'

'You were tired, Nicola,' Aunt Mary was quietly comforting. 'You've been through a lot and the journey was just too much. Now that you're here you must rest, get strong and well and then begin to enjoy yourself.'

'I—I'll be fine tomorrow,' Nicola assured her, stumbling over the words.

Blake cut into the little scene with his usual ruthless determination.

'I doubt it,' he said coldly. 'Mary is quite right, of course. I should never have sent Dolores to you. I thought you might wish to come down and join us. The last thing we want is for you to feel left out.'

'There's no chance of that, Blake,' Mary said determinedly. 'Just let her come round in her own time and then we'll really get to know her.'

'I already know her,' Blake pointed out with a certain amount of cynicism in his tone. 'I agree, though, that you need time alone with Nicola. You'll get plenty of it. There's still the film,' he finished irritably.

'Oh, dear,' sighed Mary. 'Let's hope it's able to run through smoothly now. I do believe it's jinxed, darling.'

'Just bad luck,' Blake muttered, finishing his drink. 'Looking on the bright side, though, if things had been going smoothly, I would never have had the time to get Nicola.'

She noted he didn't say fetch, bring or collect. 'Get' sounded much more sinister somehow, as if she had been netted. Her eyes went worriedly to his face and he looked at her for a minute before grimacing wryly.

'Don't panic,' he murmured darkly. 'The difficulty with the film is a separate matter. You didn't have a thing to do with it.' His eyes left hers abruptly and he put his hand on Aunt Mary's chair. 'Let's eat,' he said shortly. It was almost an order and Nicola knew he had had quite enough of small talk, especially with her.

She was not really hungry, but she forced herself to eat. It would have been very awkward had it not been for the kindness of her aunt, who kept up a steady stream of conversation, including Nicola in everything. Blake made no such attempt; he seemed to be brooding over something and Nicola had to assume that it was her.

She knew that he did not like this arrangement at all. She had known it all the time. He had brought her here because Aunt Mary wanted her but, had it been left to him, he would never have even thought of it. She was in no doubt that she did not fit into his sort of life and probably would not have fitted into Aunt Mary's had the older woman not been crippled.

Nicola was almost daydreaming, not pleasant thoughts but a sort of self-protective meandering in her mind to distance herself from Blake's hard eyes. He glanced at her very often and there was still the speculative look, an almost irritated air about him.

'I'm sorry?' Nicola suddenly realised that her aunt was speaking to her and she snapped to attention when Blake frowned rather grimly.

'I was just saying, dear, that I regret being a coward.'

'You're nothing of the sort,' Blake growled while Nicola was still trying to understand what it all meant.

'Oh, this!' Mary looked down at her lifeless legs and smiled ruefully. 'Believe me, this is nothing when you consider the time I've wasted in my life because I didn't have the courage to say I was sorry.'

'Mary, what the devil are you talking about?' Blake asked sharply. 'What have you ever done that needed words of apology?'

'Before your time, Blake,' Aunt Mary said softly, 'long before your time. Now it's too late and I suppose that's what life is all about: belated regrets.'

'You're being foolish, Mary,' Blake asserted, getting up to pour more wine. He shot a reproving look at Nicola as if she should be saying something to bring this kind of talk to an end, but she could not at all. She had no idea what her aunt meant.

'Your father and I used to be very close, Nicola,' Mary said quietly. 'It's extraordinary when you come to think of it. We were never in touch with each other in all the long years and yet, at one time, we were as close as any brother and sister could be.'

Nicola felt distressed. She had no wish to speak of her father. It brought back too much hurt, too many questions. Her mind was still asking the same thing even though she was out of hospital and in new surroundings. Why? Why? Why? Why had he started the fire? Why had he risked her life and then given his own to save her? She would never know because only he could have told her.

'Kevin, your father, was always a stickler for what was right,' Mary was continuing with a little wistful smile. 'He was my big brother. I always obeyed. Anyway, he was always right. When I married my first husband, Kevin was dubious. As it turned out, quite rightly. What caused the rift, though, was that I would be living in America.'

'I—I'm sure you had every right to—to go where your husband lived,' Nicola managed shakily, not wanting either of them to know how much this was upsetting her.

'Well, our parents were old, Nicola. Kevin thought I should stay near; after all, *he* did. We had an almighty quarrel and I stormed out. I never went back at all because my mother and father died very soon after that, long before I had got over my temper. If I had only stayed for a while,' she sighed.

'How could you have possibly known?' Nicola asked, trying to make this a sort of academic discussion to be able to keep her own sanity for the duration of the meal.

'I couldn't. The fact is and always was that I was selfish and Kevin was not. You must have been very proud of your father, my dear. He was a very special man, very honourable. I should have had the courage to write to him, to tell him that I was sorry, but I never did. I was never like him. Kevin always did what was right, what was just.'

Nicola couldn't stand it any longer. She had also thought that. Every admiring and loving thing that her aunt had said could have been taken right out of her own head, out of her thoughts. And she had been quite wrong. How could he have always done what was right? He had caused the fire that had cost him his life, the fire which had almost cost her her own life. His last-minute heroism could never atone for the fact that he had started the whole thing knowing she was asleep and defenceless in the house.

'Excuse me!' She sprang up and walked quickly to the open French windows, going out on to the curving porch and stepping down into the dark garden away from their sight.

'Nicola!' She heard her aunt's voice but she could not turn and face them.

'Leave it, Mary!' Blake's sharp command was the last thing Nicola heard and then she started to run, making for the glitter of the sea, tears streaming down her face.

Blake caught her seconds later, his arms enclosing her as he spun her round.

'The cliff!' he grated warningly and Nicola blinked the tears away, shivering when she realised she had been running straight for the rocky tumble of cliff that fell to the sea. She was almost at the edge and, even in the moonlight, she knew she would not have noticed until it was too late.

'I—I'm sorry,' she choked. 'I know I should never have left like that, but I—I couldn't...'

'Calm down,' Blake ordered quietly. 'Mary never thought. She was lost in the past and she simply forgot that the present is very much with you at this moment.'

'I've upset her,' Nicola acknowledged miserably.

'Temporarily,' Blake murmured, an edge to his voice. 'She'll wring her hands and then feverishly try to make it all up to you.'

Nicola looked up at him, quite forgetting that the arms that had caught her were still around her and, in the bright moonlight, Blake was watching her intently.

'OK now?' he asked and she nodded, her eyes drawn to the sheer drop to the sea.

'Yes. Thank you. I—I never thought about where I was going.'

'It's safe enough as long as you don't make a mad run at it,' Blake assured her tightly. 'Just pattern it into your mind. The cliff is there and nothing is about to move it.'

He was back to being cold again and Nicola felt a wave of disappointment. She carefully extricated herself from his arms. Tonight she had not felt that odd excitement when he held her. She had been too upset and it had been merely comforting. She wasn't about to linger there until the mad feeling took hold of her again. At this moment, she didn't feel the fierce awareness and it could stay like that. She would have to pattern it into her mind, like the cliff, then she would always avoid it.

'I'll go in and—and make my peace with Aunt Mary,' Nicola murmured, making the excuse to set off back to the house.

'She'll be thinking exactly the same thing,' Blake assured her, matching her pace with his. 'Let her down lightly. Tell her you felt sick or something.'

'I did,' Nicola whispered to herself.

'Why?' She was quite shocked that he had heard and she never answered. She was never going to tell either Blake or her aunt. She would rather have them think she was slightly mad. Whatever her own thoughts, she would still protect her father's memory. If there was finally a court case, at least they were well away from England. They need never know. From the police point of view it had all been settled while she was in hospital, she had escaped it. The rest would not be of worldwide importance; her father's firm was small beside other firms.

'Why did you run out, Nicola?' As they came to the porch and the lights there, Blake took her arm, swinging her to face him.

'I—I suppose I didn't want anyone to see me cry.' She muttered her excuse, dropping her head, but he tilted her face with one imperious finger.

'I've seen you cry,' he reminded her steadily. 'It didn't astonish me any. I figured you had good cause. What did Mary say that made you run?'

'Nothing,' she assured him.

'You're lying,' he said inflexibly, fixing her with unwavering eyes.

'Well, then, it—it's private.'

Her attitude made it quite clear that she would say nothing more and, for a few seconds, Blake looked at her steadily, his eyes narrowed and assessing, but nothing would have made her tell him about her heartache and he let her go, urging her into the lights of the room where her aunt sat waiting with a very anxious and regretful expression on her face.

Later, Nicola got ready for bed in a bemused state of mind. She could not have even begun to hope that her Aunt Mary would be so kind, so gentle. It felt like having a family again, although Blake was certainly not included in it.

For his part, he had simply lingered around until everything was back to normal and Nicola had not one doubt that he was there simply to see to it that her aunt was not upset in any way. He had then gone off and left them to it.

'We won't be seeing Blake for much longer, I'm afraid,' her aunt said with a sigh. 'He'll be back with that wretched film in a day or two, perhaps even tomorrow.'

'Is it going wrong?' Nicola ventured, quite awed that Blake would allow anything to go wrong.

'Not really. It seems to be jinxed.' Mary laughed rather sheepishly as she said it. 'I've been around the film people for so long that I've even picked up their superstitions. This particular film, though, has not had a smooth run. There were problems with the sets, problems with the locations and finally the big star broke her leg. Blake was going berserk. Coming to fetch you was a very good thing. It took his mind off the problems for a while at least. Janet should be able to do most of the scenes by next week.'

'Janet?' Nicola asked with interest.

'Janet Browning, dear. She's a very nice girl, such a good sport, even though she is a big star.'

Nicola was impressed. Janet Browning was a star on both sides of the Atlantic, beautiful and talented. Blake wouldn't want to get rid of her, however much money it was costing to hold up the production.

'She looks nice,' Nicola ventured and Mary nodded wryly.

'She is. If Blake is going to be mixed up with anyone in the film world, I must say I'd prefer it to be Janet. Sooner or later he's going to think about getting married and I suppose I'm selfish enough to hope it will be somebody I can take to. It's sure to be someone from his own world. Janet would be ideal.'

Nicola thought of the Janet Browning she had seen on film, tall, with dark red hair and a sort of wry smile in her eyes. Nicola had taken to her too. It would probably be someone like that who would end up being Blake's wife. Janet Browning looked as if she just might be able to cope with him.

She settled down in bed, trying to relax. It had been a rather traumatic evening and, although her aunt had been quite wonderful, she still felt the strain. She had to admit that if Blake had not been there she would have managed a good deal better. She was too much aware of him all the time now.

There seemed to be a sort of electric force that surged between them and she knew it was all coming from her. Blake was just himself. She was the one who had changed so suddenly. All the same, she thought bitterly, it was his fault. She hadn't felt funny until he had kissed her.

Even as she thought it, Nicola admitted that it was not true. She had felt funny the moment she had seen him and he had not let her escape that feeling. It was probably that she was not used to aggressive masculinity, and Blake was all of that. She sighed and closed her eyes, shutting out the moonlight that flooded into the room.

She was alone up here, very private. Blake was still in his studio, studying the first reels of film that were already prepared. Aunt Mary had told her that he had a huge purpose-built suite at the back of the house where he worked. Sometimes he slept there, apparently. Sometimes he worked all night. He would probably be working all this night if he was about to get back to the production. She fell asleep trying to imagine what he would be doing, intrigued by his importance.

Her own screams woke her up, but she could not pull out of it, could not get her eyes open at all, and she heard for the first time ever the terrifying reality of her own fear. It was like being paralysed, locked in her own body with only fear beside her. She was aware of the room, of the door crashing open, but it did nothing to release her.

Blake lifted her almost savagely, crushing her against him as he wrenched aside the bedcovers. He took her face in his hands and shouted at her with almost no pause in his actions.

'Nicola! Wake up!'

Nicola opened shocked eyes and stared at him wildly, trying to fit him into her dream, but he would not fit at all. He was real and almost as terrifying as the nightmare. The dark eyes pinned her fast and his hands round her face tightened as he watched her like a hunter.

Neither of them said anything, and it slowly dawned on Nicola that he was still dressed, only the buttons of his shirt unfastened and his tie and jacket discarded. He was sitting beside her on the bed and her legs were pressed against the strength of his thighs.

'You were dreaming again,' he said tautly and she nodded, her eyes avoiding him.

'I know. This time I heard it myself.'

'But you didn't stop.' His voice was still edged with savagery and she felt reprimanded at once.

'I couldn't. I—I didn't seem able to really wake up.'

Blake let her go and stood with one smooth movement, looking down at her and then pacing about in an irritated manner.

'How long is this going to go on?' he growled, and Nicola instantly became defensive.

'I don't do it deliberately,' she choked. 'I don't just snuggle up in bed and scream like a lunatic. I told you right from the first that I shouldn't be here. It was you who insisted, so don't go blaming me now if I'm getting on your nerves!'

'I don't have nerves!' Blake rapped out, spinning round to her, his face dark with anger. 'I was not aware that I even vaguely suggested that you deliberately entertain yourself with nightmares.'

He was glaring at her and Nicola tried to glare back, which was difficult when she was fighting off the residue of the dream and trying not to shake pitifully.

'You asked angrily how long this was going to go on and...'

'And you instantly assumed the worst,' he grated. 'It's always a good idea to assume the worst with me, but on this occasion I was thinking about you, as it happens. I should be back to work tomorrow. It occurred to me that you will then be up here alone and I can't readily come up with a solution.'

'I'll be all right,' Nicola muttered, ashamed of her bleak thoughts.

'The hell you will!' he snapped harshly. 'Once again, I just got to you in time. The last two episodes I've been very much available, especially on the plane. This time I had just come upstairs.'

'It's three o'clock,' Nicola pointed out, her face beginning to flush at his reminder of the particular episode on the plane.

'I work when I feel like it,' Blake retorted sharply, staring at her flushed cheeks and wild eyes. 'Don't start pinpointing my nasty habits or you'll not last long.'

Nicola looked away hastily and shivered as he walked to the bed and sat beside her. She wished now that she had made some sort of a move to get back under the covers. This was another of those delicate and revealing nighties he had bought her and she felt uneasy enough as it was.

'Obviously I can't put you with Mary,' he mused more quietly. 'The only other thing is to get one of the girls to sleep up here, Dolores or Angelica.'

'No!' Nicola looked up quickly, her face horrified. 'I won't have all and sundry regarding me with astonished and pitying eyes!'

'Am I pitying, Nicola?' Blake asked wryly, looking down at her with sardonic amusement. 'I must be slipping.'

'You—you're not pitying,' Nicola muttered, trying to escape the amused irony by wriggling to get into bed. 'You're—different.'

'Impartial?' His firm hand stopped her stealthy attempt to move and he tilted her face to look at her deeply. 'I'm not even that. I'm trying to solve a problem that I've helped to precipitate. I'm well aware that if I hadn't insisted on your coming here so quickly you would have been more ready to face things. The trouble is, I didn't have the time to wait and, this evening, Mary's reminiscences brought on exactly what I expected. It's therefore my problem and I have to solve it.'

'It's not your problem,' Nicola assured him in an embarrassed voice. 'It's purely my problem. You were just the go-between, in a way.'

'In what way?' His hand was still on her shoulder, detaining her, and she was becoming more aware of it every minute. It was warm, almost inviting, although what it was inviting she didn't dare to think. 'Don't you feel that I was pretty domineering as a mere go-between?'

'Well, I can understand now. It was because of Aunt Mary and I'm glad I came because she's very nice. She—she reminds me of my—my father.'

Blake just went on looking at her, his gaze thoughtful. Slowly, his eyes seemed to gain in concentration until Nicola felt she was going right into his mind. It was very quiet, although there was the faint wash of the sea, the shifting waves on the pebbles of the beach below the cliff.

'Maybe I should take you with me,' Blake murmured, almost to himself, and Nicola's eyes widened in shocked surprise.

'With you?'

'I can see that the thought alarms you,' he said drily, a spark of amusement at the back of his dark eyes. 'It would be one way to keep an eye on you. Then again, you're *supposed* to be here for Mary's sake.'

'I—I am here for her sake,' Nicola stammered. 'I'll be all right. I told you.'

'But I never believe you, Nicola,' he derided, his amusement growing. 'I keep thinking of you up here, all alone, screaming in terror and me miles away.'

'Well at least you wouldn't know,' Nicola managed shakily. 'In any case, there's nothing you can do, is there? I'm not your responsibility.'

'Why do I doubt that?' he asked ironically. 'I could give you something else to think about,' he added. 'It worked before.'

CHAPTER SIX

NICOLA didn't know what he meant until she became aware that the dark head was bending towards hers, his eyes on her trembling mouth.

'No!' She tried to pull back, but his arms were suddenly around her, holding her implacably. 'Please don't, Blake.'

'Why not?' he murmured against her lips, arching her closer.

'Because you don't mean it.'

'Would it make any difference if I did?' He never waited for an answer. Once again those devastating lips captured hers and Nicola felt herself pulled into him, made to curve against him by expert hands. Her head moved of its own volition to his shoulder as he kissed her lingeringly and, when he lifted his head, she just kept her eyes closed.

'You can come out now.' The highly amused sound of his voice brought her back to reality and Nicola blushed even more fiercely when she discovered that her body had curled against his so much that her long, slender legs were stretched across his thighs. She was almost sitting on his knee and this time, when she struggled, he let her go.

'You're a very cruel person,' she declared shakily and one dark brow rose in devastating irony.

'Show me one bruise.' Before she could answer, Blake was on his feet, the bedcovers drawn back and she was helped underneath them to some sort of security. 'It was an option,' Blake drawled sardonically. 'Let's see if it works. It just might take your mind off other things.'

'You have a staggering sense of your own abilities!' Nicola seethed, her mind outraged although her heart was thumping like mad. He looked down at her sceptically.

'The only thing staggering about me is my astonishment at your inexperience,' he growled, his eyes narrowed on her flustered and anxious looks. 'Of course, you could have landed the odd blow at my face.' His eyes were asking why she hadn't and Nicola was asking herself the same thing. Was she just going to accept this? It was something she would never have accepted before, something she would have flown into a rage about.

Her eyes glittered with annoyance. As an option to get her better it was perhaps a good thing, because she was very angry now.

'Ah!' Blake looked at her closely, his lips twisting in a tight smile. 'I struck a chord.'

'Next time,' Nicola raged quietly, 'it won't be the only thing to be struck.'

'You imagine there's going to be a next time?' he enquired quizzically. 'If an option doesn't work there's not much point in pressing the matter.'

'Goodnight!' Nicola said bitingly and he smiled again, turning to the wide open door.

'See you in the morning,' he murmured. 'Let me know how you sleep.'

'I'll sleep very well,' Nicola snapped, drawing the sheets to her chin when he turned and ran his gaze over her.

'I can believe it—now,' he said laconically, closing the door as he left.

Nicola just collapsed back against the pillows, berating herself for the way she had behaved. She should have been berating him too, but, once again, she had simply allowed the excitement to drown her. And, once again, it had been his superb acting ability, his skill.

She slid down the bed and switched off the lights he had put on as he came into the room, only then realising that, once again, the nightmare had receded completely out of sight. Even thinking about it, she couldn't force it back, although she tried hard.

Blake's kiss was too much at the front of her mind and she could still feel his hard arms around her. She could smell the tangy aftershave he used; it was mixing with her own warmer perfume, making a cocktail of almost erotic fragrances to intoxicate her senses. She shivered and struggled to bring herself back to reality. It was too hard, though, because the reality was there and not possible to dismiss.

Blake was reality. There was nothing ethereal about him. He was hard and uncompromising in everything, even taking a decision to kiss her and hold her just to see what would happen. It had been an option, an experiment because he had seen quite well what had happened on the plane.

She wondered almost hysterically if he would ask her about it in the morning, something like, 'Well, how did it go, Nicola? Were you too much aware of me to have another nightmare?' What would he do if she agreed happily that it had worked? she wondered. Would he come back every other day to top up the medicine?

She opened her eyes, glaring at the moonlight. He thought she was a simpleton! Well, she would just have to show him how wrong he was. Blake Anderson was in need of a set-down. When she saw him in the morning she would be completely aloof and she would look at him with distaste. It gave her a small amount of comfort and, in the end, she fell asleep, but not for a very long time. The excitement would not fade, even though she knew it was all play-acting.

She also knew that if any of the men she had known at college or later had behaved like that, her inclination would not have been to curl against them and swoon. It would have been to beat them black and blue. And it was no use telling herself that Blake was hard and that she was, to a great extent, at his mercy. The thought of that would never have entered her head if she had been herself. She would have acted first and worried later.

Her last anxious thought was that even if she had been her old self, it would not have made any difference to the excitement, the slowly mounting magic. She gave a small moan and hid her head under the sheets. There was a sort of chemical reaction when Blake touched her, something she had no control over, something that melted her inside, and the awful thing about it was, she was pretty certain that he knew.

In the morning, Nicola's breakfast was served to her in bed, at her aunt's orders, and she could not very well refuse it. In any case it was a very nice surprise, as if somebody cared about her. When she went downstairs later, Blake was not there and she felt a surge of irritation mixed with disappointment. She had meant to show him this morning that he was wasting his time, trying to make her look foolish, because she had decided in the bright light of day that he was doing exactly that.

Her aunt was outside, talking to the gardener and trundling about in her mechanised chair, a straw hat on her head. For all her disability, she looked healthy, and Nicola was bewildered at the great feeling of comfort it gave her to see the woman who, until yesterday, she had never even met.

'How are you, dear?' When she heard Nicola's footsteps, Aunt Mary turned and smiled at her. 'I must say you look lovely today.'

Nicola had wondered if she was a bit overdressed for simply hanging around the house. She was wearing a very expensive cotton dress in pale green, the small flowers on it softening the gentle colouring even more. It was sleeveless, flowing, another of Blake's gifts.

'You look a little like your mother,' Mary mused softly. 'I remember her. She was a beautiful woman. Kevin adored her.' She suddenly looked embarrassed and turned away, before glancing up again with a wry smile. 'There I go again, letting my tongue run away with me.'

'It's all right,' Nicola smiled. 'I can't remember her.'

'I wouldn't want to upset you again, Nicola,' Aunt Mary said quickly, adding with a sort of grin, 'anyway, Blake told me off after last night. You do look lovely, though.'

Nicola was quite sure that Blake had not told her aunt off or anything like it.

'He bought me this dress,' she said, changing the subject. 'In fact, he bought me everything.'

'Well, you lost everything, my dear. In any case, he can afford it. He's quite wealthy. There's a lot of money in films at Blake's level, so don't go feeling anxious.'

'I suppose he's already left?' Nicola ventured, alarmed when the thought made her feel very vulnerable, as if she had lost the only person she really knew, the only person she could turn to.

'Not yet. He's working. He'll be leaving today, though, I'm sure. He'll probably want to speak to you before he goes because he asked where you were when he came to breakfast. I told him very firmly that you were having a day of being pampered.'

Nicola could just imagine how he would have taken that news and she was on edge all the rest of the time, trying to become very interested in the garden and trying to keep her mind off Blake. When the inevitable happened, just before lunch, she was quite glad to face it and get it over with.

'The *señor* would like to speak with you, *señorita*.' Dolores appeared, full of smiles, and as Nicola left she saw Dolores take Aunt Mary firmly in hand. She would have to remember that this household was already running smoothly and she would have to try not to disrupt things.

She followed the directions and finally found herself outside the suite that Blake kept for himself.

'Come in!' Blake called out when she knocked, and Nicola took a deep breath and walked through the door, realising that it was taking more courage each day to face him. He was seated, watching a huge screen, and she knew that this really was the lion's den. Over their time together, she had quite forgotten his importance, but now it hit her suddenly and she felt quite inadequate, even more so when he froze the picture and the lights came up as he turned to stare at her menacingly.

'Why the devil did you knock?' he rasped, taking her by surprise.

'I—I thought . . . well—I . . .' she faltered to a halt and then glared right back at him, her sudden awe forgotten. 'Because I was taught my manners,' she snapped. 'I was entering your private domain, so naturally I knocked. In any case, I'm an intruder in the house.'

'Come here!' Blake stood and glowered at her. 'Luckily, nobody tried to teach me my manners so I can sort you out with an easy mind. You *live* here! I don't want to find that you've been creeping about like an uninvited ghost while I'm away or there'll be trouble!' he grated irritably when she walked towards him, her moment of defiance gone.

'When are you going?' Nicola asked tremulously, worried by his savage looks, but even more worried that he would be miles away, a thought that seemed to keep coming back unexpectedly.

'Right after lunch. I have a few more of these to look at and then I'll get ready.' He sank back to his seat and, when she stood there irresolute, he pointed at another comfortable-looking chair and simply said, 'Sit!'

'Did you want to speak to me?' she ventured, and he waved her to silence in that imperious manner she had grown quite accustomed to.

'Later. I didn't expect you to obey my commands so swiftly. I want to get this done before I get embroiled in anything else.'

'I can come back,' Nicola began, half standing, but his hand shot out and secured her, making her sink back into the chair. He didn't bother to make any comment. He seemed to forget that he was holding her hand but, after a second or two, he released her and pressed a switch. The lights faded slowly as he turned his eyes to the screen where the picture was already beginning to move again.

Nicola was fascinated. There was no sound and Blake frequently stopped the film and ran it back, viewing some things several times. It all looked superb to her, but as she glanced at him secretly she could see that he was not of the same opinion. He was making notes and sometimes he stopped the film and stared at it for a good while, moving it on slowly and stopping it at several frames.

When he finally switched off he looked anything but pleased and Nicola asked, 'Is that the finished film—I mean, so far. . .?'

'The rushes,' he growled. 'First prints. Sometimes it's easier to see mistakes when the thing is actually on film. Normally I see the rushes daily, but I was otherwise occupied.'

Bringing her back to California, she already knew that, and it only made Nicola feel more of a nuisance. She was left with the impression that although Aunt Mary had wanted to see her, Blake had been greatly inconvenienced. She had even disrupted his nights with her screaming.

'Aunt Mary said that Janet Browning had broken her leg,' she ventured. It was necessary to say something because Blake was still sitting, staring at the empty screen, his brows furrowed by a deep frown.

'Well, if she had to have an accident, at least it was well timed,' he muttered caustically. 'It gave me the chance to get over for the première and collect you.'

'Both of which events you could have done without,' Nicola pointed out sharply, angered by his way of ignoring her when he had specifically ordered her to come to his suite.

'Sure!' He shot her a sceptical look and then gave one of his worrying grins. 'Nothing comes easy. What do they say? When God closes a door he closes a window?'

'They do not! He opens a window! It's meant to give hope.'

'Is that a fact?' he drawled. 'I really don't know why I said it. The line about problems coming in threes is more appropriate.'

'If I'm a problem it's because you made me come!' Nicola stormed, jumping up and preparing to leave this irritating interview. 'If you hadn't been so domineering I would have still been in England and you could have viewed your—your *rushes* and gone off to rage at the poor unfortunate people who have to work with you.'

She spun round to march out, but Blake was just a little too fast for her. He stood and collected her all in one fluid movement, his arms securing her, tight and hard around her.

'Wicked temper,' he observed drily and Nicola glared up at him.

'What did you want me for?' she snapped. 'Did you want me to admire the film or have you another reason for seeing me?'

'I don't know when I'll be back,' he warned quietly, his derision dying. 'You're on your own here. I want to know what your intentions are.'

'What do you mean?' Nicola looked puzzled and he let her go, but his hands came firmly to her shoulders.

'I don't altogether trust you,' he mused, staring at her intently. 'For now, Mary is a novelty. I'm sure she'll wear off. Will you then disappear back to England and your small hotel close to the bank? I wouldn't take kindly to it.'

Nicola's shoulders sagged as the reality of her position here hit her yet again. She was living each day as it came, no plans about anything. Far from scheming to escape when he left, she had been dreading his going, and the dread came back with a rush.

'It would be difficult just to disappear,' she said uneasily, avoiding his probing eyes. 'In any case, I told you I was glad that I came. I have no intention of simply deserting Aunt Mary as soon as your back's turned. She's kind and she's all I've got now.'

'OK. I'll try to believe you. I have not forgotten, however, that you were upset when she talked about your father. I can't promise that she won't do it again.'

'I was tired and a little taken by surprise. Next time, I'll be ready for it.'

'Will you?' Blake asked quietly, tilting her face and pinning her with dark eyes. 'It's going to take some time to recover, especially as you're keeping a lot of things to yourself.'

'You know everything,' Nicola protested quickly. 'Even before you saw me, at the hospital they would have spoken to you and Dr Gregory must have...'

'Your Dr Gregory told Mary the bare facts,' Blake assured her grimly. 'He's totally on your side. As to the hospital, they told me about your condition. I know damned well that there's something else, but I didn't have the time to find out and nobody has said anything at all to ease my suspicions.'

'There's nothing,' Nicola insisted.

'No?' He cupped her face in warm, strong hands. 'I don't believe you, Nicola. You've got an extra grief that you're keeping all to yourself.'

'You can't possibly know that,' she said anxiously, and he stared at her for one more intent second before letting her go.

'No. I can't, can I? It's merely an instinctive feeling. If you're in trouble I want to know before it hits Mary. *Nothing* is going to be allowed to cause her problems, not even you.'

Of course he meant especially her, and Nicola tried to be bright and off hand.

'I'm not in trouble. I don't see how you can even begin to think that. I've already faced my troubles.' Her voice broke a little, the past tearing at her unexpectedly and she turned away to the door. 'If that's all?'

'Until I come back,' he warned. 'A little while ago I told you that you live here, and so you do—in *my* house. I control my domain and everything in it. That includes Mary's happiness and it includes you.'

'I'm not permanent,' Nicola stated, glad to reach the door and get her fingers on the handle.

'That's up to Mary,' he grunted and she simply fled. She was not going to be here for long and this idea that he was the only thing she could hang on to was quite ridiculous. She was alone.

Getting to know her aunt would be very nice, but it was merely for a few weeks. Later she would have somebody to write to, somebody who was a relative, but that was as far as it would go. Blake would put her out of his mind the moment his car pulled away from the house. That was perfectly all right too. She had a new life to build and it could not be built here.

Blake had lunch with them on the terrace that faced the sea and he was all ready to leave. Nicola tried not to feel dismayed by the thought. She had already sorted it out in her mind, but the sight of him brought back the worries and a funny feeling in the pit of her stomach that she took to be panic.

He looked very alert. For someone who seemed to be content to stay up half the night and then settle somebody's nightmare, he looked physically confident and at ease. He was wearing grey trousers and a white short-sleeved shirt that was made just slightly formal by a tie.

'Doesn't Nicola look lovely, Blake?' Aunt Mary asked with a smile at Nicola that was filled with pride. 'I never expected to have such a beautiful niece. She's got hair like pure gold.'

Blake said nothing. His eyes ran very comprehensively over Nicola, noting the shine of her hair and the slightly embarrassed flush to her cheeks. She thought he was just going to stare at her and keep silent, but he embarrassed her even more by saying,

'She'll need some more clothes. When I get back, I'll see to it.'

Aunt Mary beamed, but Nicola was back to feeling like the stray cat. She followed him into the hall when he got up to leave and her eyes were bright with annoyance.

'I don't want seeing to,' she said sharply. 'I'm not incapable.'

'You're incapable of driving into any town and sorting out what you need,' he pointed out with infuriating calm, adding, 'Which reminds me, you need some money.'

'I'm not a—a . . .'

'Kept woman?' he enquired with sardonic help-fulness, turning to face her. 'At the moment, you are. Somebody has to look after you. Who else but me?'

'You make me feel like a useless burden,' Nicola said, feeling suddenly gloomy, her temper dying as he shrugged into his jacket, tossing his car keys in his hand.

'You're not exactly useless,' he pointed out sardoni-cally. 'You're here to delight Mary.' He looked down at her with a sudden smile, a smile that reached right into his eyes. 'Get better, Nicola,' he ordered softly. He walked to the door and she stood staring after him with a very melancholy face. It was ridiculous, but she wanted to go with him very badly indeed.

He turned to look back at her and, once again, caught her off-guard, her expression very gloomy. His eyes nar-rowed thoughtfully and then the firm lips tilted into a wry smile.

'Watch that cliff,' he warned and left, and she was quite sure he was laughing at her. If she had any sense she would be laughing at herself, but instead there was a very empty feeling that was growing by the second. When his car pulled away she found herself biting her lip to stop the protest that threatened to surface. She was going to miss him badly. It was quite insane, but it was there all the same.

Over the next few weeks, Nicola got very close to her aunt. Her father was never mentioned. She knew that Aunt Mary would have liked to talk about him, to even tell her about their childhood together, and if things had been normal Nicola would have welcomed it. Things were anything but normal, though, and the subject was left strictly alone without either of them saying anything.

Nicola was surprised and pleased one morning to find that she had a letter from England, and she didn't have to open it to know it was from John Gregory. His diabolical handwriting was all she needed to see and, as she opened it, she was amused to think that somehow it had arrived, in spite of his scrawling attempt at the address.

Amusement turned to astonishment when she read it, though, because it was not in any way an excuse to gossip about her old home town.

'I had a letter from Blake Anderson the other day,' he wrote. 'He wanted to let me know that you were safe and being cared for. It was very good of him, quite surprising considering his hard reputation. I must say, it eased my mind. There are one or two things he wants me to do for him so I expect I'll be keeping in touch. Makes one feel almost part of the family.'

He then went on to tell her the latest news about the place, but Nicola hardly saw the words. All she could think of was that Blake had gone to the trouble of writing to England even though he was so busy. But the part about his wanting Dr Gregory to do one or two things for him was ominous, especially as it was so much out of character for Blake. He was utterly self-sufficient and she could not imagine the time when he would be asking favours. Unless it was something about her, some information that only John Gregory could get.

She knew it must be about her father. Blake had been suspicious and had told her so. He was not the sort of man to let things slide. What astonished her was that he had even bothered. But, then again, he was worried that something would surface that would upset Mary. It filled Nicola with dark forebodings.

She did not want him to know about her father, about the fire and about the fact that he would have been in serious trouble with the police if he had lived. It was not shame or embarrassment, but it would probably bring pity even to Blake's dark eyes. She had escaped from all that and she never wanted to see the emotion again.

It spoiled the whole morning and, in the afternoon, she left her aunt and, after many warnings to take care, she climbed down the rocky path to the wave-washed beach below the cliff. She had never ventured there before and she was glad she had come when she stood looking at the great sweep of ocean and felt the wind in her hair. It was worth the stiff climb she would have to face to get back to the top.

Nicola set off, walking by the edge of the waves, seeing that she could go quite a long way without being cut off by further rocky outcrops. It was exhilarating, soothing and, when she turned back to walk to the part of the beach below the house, she was in a better frame of mind—until she saw Blake!

He was walking towards her, his eyes steadily on her, and she instantly felt guilty, in fact her mind almost scrambled. Why was he here, back again? Was he angry about her being down by the ocean? Had he heard from Dr Gregory? She could not take her eyes from him and she had no idea that she looked anxious and vulnerable, suddenly defenceless. His dark eyes narrowed further, piercingly on her until he was close and stopped, looking down into her upturned face.

'I can tell you're wild with joy to see me,' he murmured softly. 'I knew it by the way you raced toward me, shouting my name.'

'You took me by surprise,' Nicola told him breathlessly, her green eyes searching his face for some clue as to why he was here. 'You've only been gone for a few weeks.'

'And you would have preferred a few years,' he finished ironically. 'I came back to check up on things. We don't work this weekend. Sometimes I have to let the slaves rest.'

'I—I had a letter from Dr Gregory,' Nicola told him in a rush, her eyes locked with his.

'Did you?' For a second his glance flared over her and then he turned back the way he had come, taking her arm lightly. 'So did I. I got it on location. He thanked me for letting him know how you are—English courtesy.'

He was very off-hand, but Nicola was not fooled and she hesitated to say anything else about it because clearly he didn't want to tell her what he had asked John Gregory to find out. She just fell silent and Blake let the silence hold until they were at the foot of the cliff, then he turned her to face him.

'I came back because he's due to phone me here,' he said, looking at her steadily. 'I want answers, Nicola, and I mean to get them.'

'It—it's spying on me,' she protested, her cheeks paling at his determination. He was quite prepared to leave the film in order to come back here for the one call from England and she knew John Gregory. He would tell Blake everything. This new beginning would be no beginning at all.

'I'm not spying on you!' His easy, quiet manner deserted him rapidly and his hands gripped her arms. 'I asked you to tell me and you refused. You denied that anything was wrong and I know damned well that something is wrong. One way or another, I'll find out.'

'You have no right to pry into my past!' Nicola flared, bitterness sweeping over her. 'You have nothing to do with me!'

'But I have everything to do with Mary,' he rasped, his grip on her arms tightening. 'It's quite obvious that she loved and admired your father. It's equally obvious that since I've been away she has turned all that affection on you. Since I arrived I've been bombarded about her dear Nicola. If the sky is to fall on her, I want to be there to catch it.'

'It—it's not going to—to fall on her,' Nicola managed huskily, fear suffocating her anger.

'Once again, I don't believe you,' he said coolly. 'I'm not taking the chance that you might be telling the truth.'

'If I weren't here . . .'

'But you are here,' he interrupted angrily, 'and since you are, I have to act.'

'Then I'll go home,' Nicola stated miserably, pulling away from him and turning to the climb up the cliff.

'What home?' he grated. 'You haven't a thing to go back to.'

The cruelty of that statement hit her like a physical blow and Nicola stopped, her head falling in defeat, her back turned to him as she hid her distress.

'You're wrong,' she choked. 'I have a country of my own, a life I once had, friends . . .'

Blake swore under his breath and swung her round, catching her in his arms, his hand in her bright hair.

'What friends? Where were they when you needed them? Why did they desert you? What were they too embarrassed to face?'

'Me!' Nicola cried. 'They were too embarrassed to face me. They couldn't look me in the face and say they were sorry that my father had almost killed me!'

Blake tightened her to him, his face taut.

'That's what you think?'

'It's what everybody thinks, including the police,' she said, and Blake's harsh looks softened as he looked down at her.

'He gave his life for you.'

'At the last minute and to no avail,' Nicola sobbed.

'You poor little devil,' Blake muttered and Nicola went wild, struggling fiercely, lashing out at him.

'Let me go!' she shouted. 'I don't want your pity and I don't want you prying into my life. Nothing is going to touch Aunt Mary because I'm going back home, and don't you tell me I have no home. Home is where the heart is and mine is not here and never will be. I'll go tomorrow!'

'If you went back, I would simply come and get you again,' Blake said steadily, his eyes holding hers. 'As I haven't the time, your chances of leaving are nil.'

'You can't stop me,' Nicola whispered, shuddering at the determined look on his face.

'I can and I will,' he stated implacably. 'Meanwhile, we'll go back to the house and you can get your act together before we face Mary.'

It was harder than she had thought, climbing the cliff, and her great misery did not help. Her legs were shaking and, if it hadn't been for Blake, she knew she would have been down there for ages, summoning up her courage to face the rocky climb.

'Don't go down there again,' Blake ordered when they made it to the top. 'I can just imagine you being there for hours on end. In a little while, the tide comes in and then it's dangerous.'

Nicola said nothing. At the moment it didn't seem to matter. There was not much now that she would face with dread. Everything was out in the open. John Gregory would tell Blake about the business, the insurance, everything.

CHAPTER SEVEN

BACK at the house, Blake went with her up the stairs, looking as if he thought she would simply fall back down if he wasn't behind her, and when she went into her room and turned to close the door he was still standing there, looking at her.

'I'm going to get a shower and—and pull myself together,' she whispered, unable to meet his eyes and he stepped into the room, closing the door firmly.

'Listen to me,' he ordered, his hands gripping her shoulders. 'Whatever happened, it was not your fault.'

'I know,' she sighed wearily, trying to turn away. 'Facing the consequences is all I have to do.'

'You have Mary and you have me,' he insisted harshly and she nodded unhappily.

'For now,' she agreed. 'I then have the rest of my life.'

'A long time,' he snapped, spinning her back to him. His eyes roamed over her face and he frowned. 'Mary seems to be convinced that your father was an admirable man.'

'He was,' Nicola muttered, looking at her feet. 'I still can't believe it.'

'Then it's not true,' Blake stated emphatically.

Nicola took a shuddering breath and looked up at him.

'The fire was started deliberately, there was no doubt about that. The—the police said that...' Her voice shook too much to continue and Blake relaxed his tight hold on her arms.

'Leave it,' he said more gently. 'Get your shower and come downstairs.'

111

'All right.' She just said it dully, obediently and Blake cupped her face in his hands, his probing gaze frustrated before his lips covered hers quickly and fiercely, taking her by surprise. His determination overwhelmed her and she made no move to resist. Her mouth fused with his readily as her hands crept to his waist and clung there. He kissed her deeply until warmth seeped back inside her and, when he let her go, she was almost swaying on her feet, her eyes closed.

'And *that* was real!' he said in a low, voice. 'Now fight back, damn you! Don't just let yourself go under when life strikes at you. You've got instincts; believe them!'

He left, slamming the door and Nicola almost staggered as she went to the shower. As usual, Blake had turned her world upside-down. Was he right? Had there been a mistake? Had her lifelong faith in her father been justified, after all? Maybe they would never know, but she felt a slight flicker of hope and it was just because Blake had said so.

She knew he wanted to do this so that Mary would never have cause to be even more regretful. But he was right, her illness and her shock had swamped her instincts, but they had been there all the time, this disbelief that her father would endanger her.

As to the kiss being real, she smiled ruefully, it wasn't and she knew it. With Blake it was a means to an end, as most things were. He was on her side, though, even if it was only for Aunt Mary's sake, and having him on her side gave her a surge of strength. The great Blake Anderson! Nicola gave a shuddering laugh and got ready, knowing she could face the evening after all, even if Dr Gregory rang with bad news. Right now, she felt that Blake would merely shout at him and tell him to try again if things were not as he wanted them to be.

When she went down, there was nothing on Blake's face to show that anything at all had happened. He was so normal that, after a while, Nicola would have believed that she had dreamed everything, except that she was waiting for the phone to ring, her mind swinging between dread and hope.

'Don't you think Nicola looks better?' Aunt Mary asked as they sat to dinner, and Nicola got the full force of Blake's scrutiny as his eyes swept over her. It was like being in the centre of dark, glittering lights and she looked away quickly as his glance lingered on her breasts and the slender length of her neck.

'She doesn't look frail and worn out any more,' he conceded. 'She's catching the sun nicely, too. Don't encourage her to think she's better, though, or you may find that your niece is contemplating deserting you. Nicola frequently mentions home.'

'Oh, you're not thinking about going back, Nicola?' Aunt Mary said quickly, her hand covering Nicola's. 'It's so lovely having you around.'

'Well, I'm not going back yet,' Nicola assured her. She was not avoiding Blake's eyes now. Her own eyes were searching his face, her expression puzzled. Why had he said that, when only a little while ago he had stated very firmly that if she left he would simply bring her back?

She was still puzzling it out when Angelica came in to say that Blake was wanted on the telephone, and Nicola forgot about the big puzzle. She was sure it would be Dr Gregory and her heart accelerated as Blake glanced keenly at her and then left the room.

He had left her with a problem, too, because all the time he was out, her aunt was pressurising her to stay and Nicola had to state very categorically that she had no intention of leaving yet before Mary was satisfied.

At least it kept her mind partially in the room and Blake seemed to be a very long time.

When he came back he said nothing, of course. Mary never expected it. She naturally assumed it was to do with his work and Blake was content to let her believe that. His eyes met Nicola's and, although his expression gave nothing away, she knew it had been his call from England.

'How do you feel about managing without Nicola for a few days?' Blake asked later, when they were having coffee.

'I would hate it!' Mary said it with a laugh, and her eyes turned to Blake questioningly. 'If it's for her own good, though, I don't mind,' she assured him.

'It's for *my* good,' Blake muttered, standing to pour more coffee. 'Things are in a muddle. I've got Janet back but now two more people are off. Luckily they're not members of the cast, but it's damned annoying. I need Nicola to take notes, pass messages, remind me of the things I've forgotten. I need a general factotum.'

Nicola was stunned. She didn't manage to say anything at all but Mary was delighted.

'Why, she'll just love it!' she exclaimed. 'She'll be able to see exactly what you do. I didn't know you were a secretary, dear,' she added, turning to Nicola. 'Of course, I never asked. I didn't want to remind you of...'

'She's not a secretary,' Blake interrupted. 'She's a computer whizz-kid. She therefore has a logical, assessing mind. She can assess my problems.' He looked at Nicola for the first time, his eyes narrowed and insistent. 'How about it?' he asked quietly. 'Do you fancy helping me out, facing my constant bad temper and everybody else's hysterics?'

Nicola knew she had to say yes and say it enthusiastically. Whatever message those eyes were giving her would be told later. This was for her aunt's benefit and she managed a bright smile.

'I'd love to! It sounds exciting!'

Blake's lips twisted ironically and she wondered if she had overdone it a bit, but Aunt Mary seemed to notice nothing amiss and Blake just nodded in a satisfied manner.

Nicola couldn't wait to get out after that because she knew he would tell her when they were alone. How had he known about her work if Dr Gregory hadn't told him? It *must* have been a call from England. She bit at her lip and began to worry, stopping that rather smartly when Blake frowned at her. His expression said quite clearly that she must keep up the act until Mary was not there.

He didn't seem to be hurrying either and, finally, Nicola escaped to her room, hoping that this would force his hand and make him come to speak to her. She wanted to know what had happened with a terrifying urgency. Blake had given her hope and she dreaded that hope being crushed now.

When he knocked later, she opened the door in a great rush and stared at him anxiously, her eyes searching his face for some clue.

'For God's sake, close your eyes,' Blake growled, walking in and shutting the door. 'They're dazzling me. Pretty soon I'm going to feel faint.'

'What did he say?' Nicola asked breathlessly, wanting to shake him.

'How do you know it was Gregory?' Blake murmured, his eyes still on her face, and she almost stamped in exasperation.

'*Please*, Blake!'

'The fire was definitely started deliberately,' he said slowly, standing with his hands in his pockets and looking at her intently. 'Whatever they said to you when you were ill, the police are still interested. They haven't closed the file.'

'They—they told John Gregory?' Nicola asked in a whisper, her face going pale.

'On the quiet. He knows one of the big noises and I asked him to snoop about.'

'Oh, he'll just love doing that,' Nicola said tremulously. 'He's a natural busybody.'

'I also asked him to find a firm of reliable private investigators,' Blake continued. 'I want action.'

Nicola's head shot up in alarm, her eyes growing enormous again. He was turning things over, probing relentlessly. Suppose . . .?

'Have faith,' Blake ordered quietly. 'Whatever the truth, we want to know it.'

'You do,' she whispered and his hands came down on her shoulders.

'So do you,' he assured her firmly. 'You'll never get over it until you know the truth. You'll never have the chance to live until everything is completely out in the open.'

She nodded and looked down rather helplessly. He was quite right, of course. She had to know the truth. The stronger she became, the more her mind asked questions and the more it refused simply to believe what she had been told.

'Why do you want to take me with you?' she asked suddenly, her eyes raised to meet his. 'Aunt Mary may have been fooled by your desperate plight, but I wasn't.'

'Damn! I thought I did it rather well,' Blake said, his lips twitching with laughter. 'Maybe you know me better than I thought.'

'I know you wouldn't need me,' Nicola stated emphatically. 'I'll be in the way.'

'No. You'll be out of the way,' Blake corrected. 'We're moving our sphere of operations from this house and well away from Mary. If anything happens she's not even going to know. In future, anyone who wants to get in touch with us does so...'

'Where we're "at"!' Nicola finished for him and he grinned down at her.

'Right. You're getting the picture. As for being in the way, I'm sure I can put your talents to good use. A brain is a brain. It all depends how you use it.'

'Dr Gregory told you about me,' she surmised and he nodded in amusement.

'He was all for telling me about your childhood ailments, describing your first steps and sending me snaps of your schooldays. I had to be firm.'

Knowing Dr Gregory, Nicola wasn't sure if this was true or not and her face flushed rosily.

'Have you noticed how much time I spend in your bedroom?' Blake murmured, adding to her confusion. 'When we get to the location, I must make sure you have a hotel miles away from me. People will talk otherwise.'

'Am I really going with you?' Nicola asked, determined not to be drawn into this type of conversation.

'Tomorrow.' He held her at arm's length and inspected her dress. 'You'll need some casual clothes. We'll get them on the way.'

'You can't keep buying me things,' Nicola protested, but he looked at her ironically and then turned to the door.

'You work for me now. I have a double hold on you. Any insubordination and I'll simply roar. It's my usual way of going about things.' He stopped and looked at her, catching the rather dazed expression on her face. 'Any nightmares?' Nicola shook her head vigorously, not trusting herself to speak, and his eyes flared over her like dark lightning. 'What did I tell you? It worked. Maybe we should measure it out—therapeutically,' he finished softly as he left. He hadn't needed to tell her what he was talking about. She knew perfectly well and, in spite of the unusual things that had happened this evening, it was the memory of Blake kissing her that lingered in her mind.

They left next morning and Aunt Mary was as excited as if she was going herself.

'It makes me feel that you're really part of the family,' she whispered, giving Nicola a hug as she bent to say goodbye. 'Anyway,' she confided, 'if Blake needs you, he's not likely to let you go back to England. He can be quite ferocious when it comes to getting his own way.'

Nicola knew that but she was not worried. Whatever her aunt thought, Nicola knew quite well why she was going with Blake.

They were going north and, on the way, they stopped for an early lunch. Blake insisted right then on buying Nicola casual clothes.

'You can't hang around a film location in silk,' he said curtly when she once again protested. 'It's not as glamorous as it seems when the finished product is viewed by the public. It's either jeans or shorts and a sweater for the evenings. Besides,' he added caustically, 'I want you to be inconspicuous.'

Nicola didn't have to work hard to fathom that one out. He meant that she was not going to do any job at all. He had just been getting her out of the way and, now that he had succeeded, she could well imagine that she would be ignored, left to her own devices and looked at with astonishment if his eyes should happen to fall on her.

Long before they reached San Francisco, they turned off the main highway and Nicola tried not to show her disappointment. Blake knew though. There was not much that escaped his keen-eyed attention.

'You'll see it,' he promised crisply. 'At the moment, I don't have time to make a detour to satisfy your curiosity. We're behind schedule and time is money.'

'Which goes to show,' Nicola muttered, 'just how many times you say things you don't mean?'

Her rather tart comment had him taking his eyes from the road for a second to look at her.

'Such as?' he enquired coolly.

'You said if I left you would simply go to England and collect me,' she reminded him. 'Obviously you wouldn't have been able to spare the time, time being money!'

'Some things are more precious than money,' he told her quietly and she knew what he meant. Aunt Mary was more precious; her peace of mind was all-important to Blake.

'She must have been a wonderful stepmother,' Nicola mused aloud, and once more Blake shot her a glance, this time of astonishment.

'What the hell is your peculiar mind pondering now?'

'I'm thinking of Aunt Mary, of course. About her peace of mind being more precious than money.'

Blake shook his head in exasperation and got on with the driving, but not before he had aimed words at her that silenced her for quite a while.

'On the subject of peace of mind,' he drawled, 'I wouldn't refuse a medical report on a piece of your mind. Of course, it would be a waste of money because I know what it would say: one word—"obtuse".'

When she spun round to glare at him his lips twisted in a peculiar smile, although he never took his eyes off the road. 'How do you know I didn't mean that you are more precious than money?' he asked softly.

'Because I know exactly what you think of me,' Nicola managed in an embarrassed voice. 'I'm a necessary nuisance!'

'Well, there is that,' he agreed. 'I can't actually deny it, being a very truthful character.' He said nothing else and neither did Nicola and the next time she risked a look at him he was just doing what he frequently did, frowning alarmingly at the inoffensive road. She would never understand Blake and she knew it was very dangerous even to try.

The town they came to quite surprised her. They had seemed to be moving into the mountains, the area sparsely populated but suddenly there was a town and it was not long before Blake stopped, the car cruising to a halt in front of a small but smart hotel.

'Here we are,' he informed her, getting out and glancing around with that air of impatience she had become used to. 'As you can see, I'm working fairly close to home this time.'

'You're filming in the town?' Nicola asked, getting out and looking around for signs of cameras and film people.

'No, several miles away,' Blake muttered, moving to get her luggage. 'We're using this hotel because it's the best and nearest.'

'So you all stay here?' Nicola asked, recognising her feeling of relief that she would not be alone among strangers.

'I don't. Most of the cast are here, though. I use the trailer. It's more convenient and keeps everyone out of my hair. After a day on location I can manage very well without irritated people making irritating suggestions.'

She knew what he meant by a trailer, it was what English people would have called a caravan, but Nicola knew that these trailers were quite spectacular and she also knew, thanks to television, that they were much used by the film industry. Some of the stars used them. They were dressing-rooms, make-up stations and anything else that they were needed for. Gloom began to descend. If

Blake used a trailer she would not see him very much, or even at all.

He took her arm and led her inside and Nicola wanted to stop and ask him plenty of questions, but almost at once they were captured by some of the people he had obviously been thinking about when he had mentioned irritation.

'Blake! In the morning I'd like to do that last take all over again.' One of the men accosted Blake immediately, planting himself squarely in their way and Nicola couldn't help but feel astonished at his temerity, considering the look on Blake's face.

'Maybe,' Blake grunted, moving forward and taking Nicola with him. It was quite clear that he would mow down anyone who stood there delaying him and a path cleared at once, although one or two people still muttered questions which Blake ignored.

'Oh, you're back!' Nicola looked up at the sound of a very beautiful voice and found herself facing a very beautiful woman. 'I drove out to the location this morning, Blake, and there'll be no problem with the steps, I went up and down a few times.'

It was Janet Browning and this time Blake's attitude was very different. He stopped and a smile actually came to his forbidding face.

'Look, Janet, I told you we could leave that for later,' he said quietly, but he got a very cheery grin.

'No need. I managed well enough. It will tidy things up and get it off your back.' She was looking at Nicola with an unspoken question in her eyes and Blake seemed suddenly to remember that he was not alone.

'Oh, this is Nicola,' he acknowledged, glancing down at her as if she had quietly materialised at his side. 'Nicola Rogers. She's Mary's niece.'

'Wait a minute,' Janet Browning laughed, shaking Nicola's hand. 'I'm trying to work out what that makes her to you.'

'Normally, a liability,' Blake said sardonically, looking down at Nicola. 'Right now, though, I'm hoping she'll be my shield and buffer, my right-hand man.'

'That means he'll yell at you first,' Janet pointed out with her eyes smiling into Nicola's. 'Did he make that quite clear? If you're getting paid, go for big money because you'll earn every cent.'

'I never shout at her,' Blake lied pleasantly. 'Mary would kill me.'

He led Nicola off to the desk, collecting her keys after the formalities were over and urging her up the long staircase. Apparently there was no lift, but then, it was a very small hotel.

Nicola was rather dazed, slightly smarting after the way he had spoken of her as if she was a sort of mindless thing he had collected *en route*. She was also pondering about his attitude to Janet Browning and comparing it with his only just civilised attitude to everyone else. Of course, Aunt Mary imagined that if he married anyone it would be Janet. It made her realise that she was merely on the edge of his world.

Over the time, she had become quite used to being with him, fatalistic about the way he kissed her and her reaction to him. Now she felt sadly left out and rather frighteningly alone.

'Here it is,' Blake announced, opening a door and then handing her the keys. 'Be it ever so humble, it's all we've got.'

Nicola didn't think it was humble. It was a very nice room, nothing, of course, to compare with her rather palatial room at Blake's house, but it was cosy and warmly furnished, clinically clean in the American manner, and she sat rather abruptly on the bed.

'What do I do all day?' she asked, looking up at him. 'Is it too far for me to walk out to where you'll be working? I wouldn't mind watching and seeing how things happen.'

'You are a source of constant astonishment to me,' Blake told her, staring down at her upturned face. 'You could well become the bane of my life, the cross I have to bear. Unravelling what you've just said, I can only conclude that you imagine this trip is a neat little lie to get you away from Mary. Now, of course, I'm going to abandon you and get about my business while you sit here and die of boredom.'

'Well, I know you didn't mean anything you said and how could you?' Nicola managed hastily. 'I quite understand why you brought me away and I actually approve. Now we're here, though, I really would like to see how you work.'

'You're going to hear how I shout pretty soon,' Blake growled. 'A few minutes ago you heard me telling Janet why you were here. Did you think I made that up so that she would be less suspicious when I came upstairs with you? You'll be on location with the rest of the slaves, bright and early tomorrow morning.'

'But how will I get there?' Nicola wanted to know. She jumped up and looked more excited than she wished to look, but it was suddenly very thrilling. 'You said you didn't stay here. I'll be stranded.'

'There's transport,' Blake assured her with an exasperated look about him. 'Everybody is collected and brought out at one time, whether they're ready or not. Breakfast will be about five in the morning and at five-thirty the wagons roll. There's a check-list and, before I leave here tonight, you'll be on it. If they forget you, you won't have to be close to hear me roar.'

'You—you mean you really need me?' Nicola asked, and his hand curled round her face, his long fingers tilting her chin.

'I really need you,' he agreed, his dark eyes amused. 'Mind you,' he added with a taunting look, 'if your intelligence doesn't match up to Gregory's boasts, you'll end up making the coffee.'

'I wouldn't mind,' Nicola assured him breathlessly. 'Just as long as I can be there and—and see... everything.'

'What you mean is that you want to make sure that I'm as unpleasant as they all say,' Blake murmured. 'I am. You'll not be disappointed.'

He let her go and turned to the door and she almost felt like grabbing his sleeve.

'Will I see you? I mean, will you still be here later?'

'I plan to spend the rest of the day with you,' he said, giving her an ironic look. 'Freshen up and get into some jeans. I'll be back for you in about twenty minutes.'

Nicola couldn't help the look of pleasure that flew across her face and he looked at her steadily for a second before he left.

'You've got dangerously expressive eyes,' he murmured, his tiger grin coming back when she looked away, her face flooding with colour, and she would have given anything just to be able to laugh it off. The trouble was, she couldn't. Blake was beginning to drive the thought of anything else right out of her mind.

When he came to collect her, it was to take her out for a drive and she soon found out why. They were filming about an hour's drive away, very close to the sea in an old settlement that seemed to have been abandoned many years ago.

'It's perfect for this part of the film,' Blake pointed out as he stopped the car and invited her to step outside. It was hot, dusty, and the wind that blew from the sea swirled around everything. There was an old church, very Spanish-looking, only the outer shell still standing, but Nicola thought she recognised the steps that Janet had been talking about. There were plenty of them, going up quite steeply to the old thick door of the ruined church.

'This was once a prosperous place—mining,' Blake told her, his eyes roaming round the area. 'It was a long time ago, though, in the last century. I wouldn't like to think what sort of a life they had then.'

'Is it a costume film?' Nicola asked guilelessly, and he slanted her a look of amused exasperation.

'Would I do such a thing?' he asked in a wryly pained voice. 'I can see you've never been to one of my films.'

'I have!' Nicola insisted, feeling pretty stupid when he looked at her like that. 'I haven't missed one so far. I just thought that perhaps you were having a change, or something.'

'This is where a very vicious criminal hides out,' he informed her, walking about and looking at the old buildings. 'It's supposed to be exactly what it is, old and derelict, a good place to go to ground. We could perhaps have got something better, but not without having people hanging around gaping at us, walking in all the wrong directions and generally getting underfoot. We've already done the studio work and the scenes in the city. This is the last leg and a couple of weeks will see the whole thing wrapped up.'

'Are you behind with filming?' Nicola wanted to know, suddenly feeling guilty about the time that Blake had spent on her.

'Not much. In spite of the fact that one crisis after another has hit the production, we're pretty much on schedule, always assuming that nothing further goes wrong.'

'You haven't really time to delve into my affairs,' she murmured almost to herself. 'It must be very galling to you when you've got so many things to do. And anyway,' she went on thoughtlessly, 'you're too important to...'

'Oh, I'm very important,' Blake said sardonically. 'I terrify people.'

'You don't terrify Janet Browning,' Nicola blurted out. 'It—it's easy to see that she means a lot to you.'

'She's a damned good actress,' Blake growled, turning her towards the sea. 'Contrary to the general belief, I do not go out of my way to upset the cast. Stupidity annoys me, however.'

He meant her, Nicola assumed, but she said nothing at all. He seemed to be angry again and she had only spoken of Janet Browning because she wanted to know if Aunt Mary's speculations were true. Not that Blake would have told her. If he had any plans, she would be the last to know.

Just away from the sand, a long row of trailers stood and her speculations about their size and luxury were confirmed as Blake led her to one and unlocked the door. He raised his hand in greeting to an older man who came out of a trailer some way off.

'Our security guard,' Blake murmured as Nicola looked surprised. 'And this is my refuge,' he added rather testily, as he opened the trailer door. 'This is where I eat, sleep and rage in silence.'

Inside it was quite luxurious and Nicola was hardly listening to him. She was very much aware that he was pointing out that this place was out of bounds to everyone, including her. She was also aware that as each day's filming finished, she would be transported to the hotel and left just like everyone else. Maybe Janet came out here? She had a car, apparently, because she had mentioned driving out.

Without warning, Nicola felt thoroughly miserable and she knew why. She wanted to be with Blake herself. She didn't want to think of him here, alone, with Janet.

'Want a coffee?' Blake asked, his mood changing from the tight irritation he had been showing, but she shook her head, even managing a slight smile.

'No, thank you. I wouldn't want to intrude for long. I mean—this is a very private place, isn't it?'

'Well, it is at the moment,' Blake agreed, leaning against the open door and watching her anxious face. 'At the moment, we're here alone. Tomorrow it will be just another office until everyone leaves.'

'How will we get any message?' Nicola asked, shooting a quick look at his strong, dark face. 'I—I mean if Dr Gregory or anyone finds something to tell you?'

'They phone the hotel. I've given that number. I've also told the desk that any calls for me when I'm not there are to be directed to you.'

'Won't people think that's funny?'

'Hilarious,' he murmured sarcastically. 'They're already looking at you with a great deal of speculation, or didn't you notice?'

'They know I'm Aunt Mary's niece,' Nicola muttered, avoiding his eyes.

'So? That's supposed to stop me? I have a reputation to keep up.'

'Janet will tell them how wrong they are,' Nicola said quickly, her breathing tight and painful. Why was he doing this, making her feel strange? Why was he standing there blocking the way out, looking tall and intimidating with his eyes slanting over here like black diamonds?

'A good reason for them to speculate even further,' he murmured darkly. 'Film people like a touch of scandal. As to Janet, they know she's invariably on my side.'

'Why?' Nicola asked almost in a whisper. 'Why is she always on your side?'

'Now why do you think?' he murmured wryly and she felt the colour flooding into her cheeks. She made a nervous little sound in her throat and tried to be very sophisticated.

'Don't ask me,' she said calmly, even though her voice had a tremor. 'I don't know the film world. I don't know if it's usual to have a mistress or two.'

'Oh, it's usual.' He was watching her with a sort of intent speculation on his face and she was very much aware how alone they were here, the guard a long way off.

'Hadn't we better be going?' Nicola asked hurriedly, trying to pass him and escape to the outside. She did not manage it. His arms captured her and he smiled down at her, his glance filled with derision.

'Let me go, Blake. Please!' she gasped anxiously. The moment he held her she wanted to turn her face up to be kissed and she knew it was a sort of madness.

'You're scared,' he murmured and she struggled hopelessly.

'Of course I'm not! Now, will you please stop amusing yourself at my expense?'

'I'm not amused, honey,' he said softly. 'I'm quite fascinated, though. Your green eyes are getting bigger again. You're still like the kitten I found. Is this where I get scratched?'

CHAPTER EIGHT

BEFORE she could move, his dark head bent to hers and his lips trailed over her cheeks, gently and slowly, giving her plenty of time to struggle more. His hands moved over her back, warmly, comfortably, and when his fingers traced the vulnerable tenderness of her nape Nicola no longer wished to struggle. Her body softened, became acquiescent and Blake drew her closer, his mouth finding hers and hardening in masculine triumph when she made no move to avoid his kiss.

This time, his kiss went further, deeper, his tongue running along her lips in a silent command, ordering them to part and, when they did, his tongue moved to the dark warmth inside, slowly and secretly exploring. His hands moved over her with slow, sweeping strokes, touching her as he had never touched her before and her body began to tremble as she moved closer, melting towards him.

Blake's hand slid to her hips, holding her sensuously against his powerful body, while his other hand speared into her hair. The kiss deepened endlessly and Nicola could hardly breathe for the wild feelings that were growing inside her. Heat was growing like the fire in her dreams, relentless flames that urged her to submit.

She was vaguely aware that he had reached out and closed the door, but it only slightly penetrated her mind. Her arms wound round his neck and his hand ran down her spine with enough pressure to force her into the hard cradle of his hips. His own arousal was obvious and

Nicola moved with innocent submission, softening to his hardness, making his hands tighten on her almost cruelly.

He had no need to hold her fast now and his hands rose to close over her breasts, his fingers seeking the hard centres and urging them to stinging life, the intimacy making her gasp against his lips.

'Why are you doing this to me?' she whispered shakily when at last he lifted his head with every sign of reluctance, his breathing as unsteady as her own.

'Surely you should be asking why I'm letting you go?' he enquired in a curiously deepened voice. His arms were back around her, but now that she could see his face Nicola knew she had to fight off the raging feelings inside. He was simply playing with her emotions, even though he knew how raw those emotions were.

'I already know why,' she said tremulously. 'It was just another display of expertise, not real. Of course you're letting me go. I'm nothing to you.' She made herself face him and a swift flare of anger crossed his face as his hands tightened.

'I thought we'd agreed that it was never real?' Blake rasped, his eyes burning down at her. 'Tonight you'll be alone. Maybe I thought you needed medication.'

'Don't!' Nicola cried bitterly, tearing herself away, opening the door and almost stumbling down the steps and into the open air. He caught her almost immediately, spinning her round and holding her fast.

'Why?' he asked harshly, going back to her question. 'You want to know why? It's because you ask for it every time I'm near. Surely you know what I'm like? You knew it even before you met me. Look at me as you do with your cat-green eyes and I'll take what I want eventually.'

'You don't want anything!' Nicola said with the same lingering bitterness. 'It's just an act, like everything else, the way you teach your new actresses.'

'Is it?' Blake snapped. 'Did it feel like an act?' Her face flushed at this reminder of his arousal and he let her go, turning to the car. 'I don't feel inclined to teach you anything,' he grated, 'although you could do with a few lessons.'

'Like how to be experienced?' Nicola seethed, her whole body trembling with shame.

'Like how to protect yourself from somebody like me,' Blake corrected acidly. 'There are several men in that hotel who would not be averse to helping you with experience. Just keep away from them, all of them.'

'Perhaps I'll enjoy it!' Nicola stated in a challenging voice, her head held high although she felt small and insignificant.

'And perhaps I'll break a few necks!' Blake snarled, opening the car door and almost pushing her inside. 'Make no mistake, I'll be watching, and if I don't like what I see, all hell will break loose!'

When they reached the hotel, Blake's temper had not at all improved, although he had control of his voice, the thick, angry sound gone, an icily cold tone taking its place.

'I'll see you at dinner,' he said shortly, when they went into the foyer. 'You'll know when it is; there being only our lot here, they hit a damned gong.'

He walked off and left her and Nicola went to get her key, managing to keep a tight control of her face until she had made it to her room. Then she just sat and trembled. She was quite frightened—scared, as Blake had surmised, because she knew that she had not one defence against him.

There was this fierce sexual recognition, a feeling she had never had before. She wanted him to hold her, to kiss her. She wanted to be able to let her eyes roam over him as his dark, intense eyes often roamed over her. She wanted him to tell everyone here that she was with him and not just Aunt Mary's niece. It was madness!

When the gong duly sounded and Nicola went down to dinner, having changed into one of her silk dresses, she found Blake standing at the bar, his head close to Janet Browning's. He was laughing, no sign of temper about him at all, and a feeling she had never had before in her life shot through Nicola. She recognised it with no doubts. It was jealousy and, when Janet saw her and motioned her forward, she went on very reluctant legs, her eyes avoiding Blake's, her mind assessing how very differently he behaved with Janet. But, of course, he would do if he was going to marry her.

The meal was a trial to her because she was sitting facing Blake and, try as she might, her eyes were drawn to him. She noticed the way his hands moved, how graceful they were, how strong-looking. The lights were picking up the dark shine of his hair, his thick black lashes casting unbelievable shadows on his high cheekbones.

In a very masculine way, he was harshly beautiful, not one sign of softness about him until he smiled. He smiled often, but it was always at Janet, and Nicola watched his lips, remembering how they had felt against her own, remembering until she felt quite faint.

'Are you all right, Nicola?'

Janet's sudden question had her looking up guiltily to find Blake's eyes on her too, his gaze narrowed and angry as if he had been aware of her awe-stricken scrutiny.

'Nicola has been very ill,' he said tightly before she could answer. 'I'll not be making her work like a slave.'

'You'll be keeping that for us,' one of the men said with a laugh, and Blake shot him one of those looks he could throw like weapons.

'More than likely,' he said caustically. 'In any spare minutes, I'll be keeping an eye on Nicola. If anything happens to her, her Aunt Mary will blame me and, of course,' he added with a certain air of menace that was not lost on the others, 'I'll blame everyone else.'

'Don't you always, Blake, darling?' Janet asked with a happy laugh, and Nicola assumed that she was either just too nice to hear any innuendoes or she was quite used to this sort of thing.

Nicola wasn't used to it and, as soon as the meal was over, she slipped off unnoticed. Not completely unnoticed, though, as she found when she made her way up the stairs.

'In the morning, you'll need something warm to wear,' Blake's unforgiving voice warned her and, when she turned, he was standing just at the bottom of the steps. 'It's cold out there until the sun gets going.'

'I'll remember, thank you,' Nicola said quietly and that sceptical smile tilted his lips.

'Thank you?' he asked ironically. 'For what? For scaring you to death? I'm very good at that sort of thing. Let's hope your nerve holds out, because you're with me now and no other help is to hand—none that I'll allow.'

He walked off without a backward glance and Nicola noticed he did not leave the hotel. He went back to Janet and, after standing rather forlornly for a second, Nicola ran up to her room, locked the door and prepared for bed. It was all going to be hurtful, something she was not sure she could face. Her mind told her she had faced worse, but right at that moment she wasn't at all certain if that was true.

It was barely light when everyone gathered for an early breakfast next morning and Nicola felt a wave of dismay when she realised that Janet Browning was not there. She did not have to be very intelligent to know that Janet had spent the night with Blake. In any case, it was no surprise. He had as good as admitted that there was something between them.

When the transport arrived to collect them she sat by herself, feeling lost and lonely. Last night she had not deteriorated into the world of nightmares. Small wonder when the present held her more closely than the past, her mind searching for Blake all the time when it had searched for the answer to the puzzle of her father's actions. Perhaps today they would hear? No. It was too soon. Today she would be with Blake, but he would probably ignore her.

At first, he did. It was quite cold by the sea, a heavy mist lying over the water, the rather eerie silence only broken by the mutters of the cast and crew as they stepped down from the bus and felt the chill of the air. The ruined church looked ghostly, wreathed in swirling strands of mist, mysterious, spectral, more the setting for a story from the past than for a modern crime thriller.

Nicola shivered, even though she had taken Blake's advice and wrapped up warm, but the atmosphere was quickly dispelled as the cast disappeared into various trailers to get ready and the camera crew began to set up their equipment for the day. Things appeared as if by magic and Nicola found herself standing around helplessly as people who knew exactly what they were about turned the abandoned, eerie place into a film set.

'Where's Janet?' Blake's voice cut coldly across the other sounds and everyone stopped, looking round helpfully.

'Thought she was with you,' the driver said with a worried look at Blake's thunderous face.

'And how did you imagine she'd managed that?' Blake grated sarcastically. 'An early morning walk, perhaps?'

His further acid comments were halted as a car came tearing into view and, seconds later, Janet stopped and came across to Blake.

'Say nothing,' she begged with a wry laugh. 'I over-slept. Luckily I had the car.'

'Lucky for you,' Blake growled. He glanced up, the first time he had even looked at Nicola, and he caught her completely off-guard as usual, her expression of relief that Janet had not spent the night with him written clearly on her face. His lips tightened and, for a second, he stared at her furiously, a black frown etched on his face. Then he turned away and ignored her.

'Tide's turning.' The information was given to Blake almost curtly and his dark glance turned to the water.

'OK.' His eyes narrowed and he nodded, still looking at the slowly lifting mist. 'What have we got, twenty minutes?'

'Thereabouts. Thirty at the most.'

'Places!' Blake called and there was instant movement, everyone ready with little fuss. Nicola had not noticed what was happening until now. She had been too absorbed with her own thoughts, but she could see that things were about to happen and she wondered where she should be. Blake would probably refuse to speak to her.

'Notebook!' he shouted and the order was passed on rapidly, the tone of his voice bringing forth a harassed-looking girl with the necessary object in her hand. She looked desperately from Blake to Nicola and Blake took it with a look of extreme exasperation and handed it across.

'What do I write?' Nicola began nervously and Blake snapped a look at her that would have frozen boiling water.

'Everything I tell you.' He moved to sit down and then glared even more as he realised that Nicola was standing and had nothing to sit on. 'Chair!' he roared and this time, almost before the words had been passed on, the girl appeared with a chair and put it hastily by Nicola.

'Does she have a sack full of everything necessary?' Nicola asked with a very shaky laugh.

'She'd better have!' Blake snarled. 'Write when I tell you and move when I move. If I find myself talking to thin air, you're back at the hotel!'

He turned his gaze on the production and Nicola didn't venture into sound again. She was cold, worried and felt utterly useless, like a child being given something to occupy her time, and Blake's mind just left her. He was doing his job and the whole unit moved like a well-oiled machine that obeyed his every command.

He was never still either, often moving to put people physically into the place he wanted them to occupy. They went through everything time after time, meticulously getting every action perfect and, all the while, Blake's eyes returned again and again to the rising mist.

Nicola followed wherever he went and soon felt no cold at all. From time to time he snapped out commands to her without even turning his head, and she would not have dared miss anything. She was almost breathless with anxiety, darting behind him and round him like a small terrier.

Frequently her mind asked her why she was doing this, why she was obeying like a simpleton. She was a computer whiz-kid. Hadn't Blake said so? The irritating thought didn't help much, though. Blake had dragged her into his life and she knew she was trying almost frantically to be part of it.

'Perfect mist!' Blake's deputy was right by them and he shot the information at Blake urgently.

'Right!' Blake strode back to his chair and it was the signal for everyone. He looked round with narrowed eyes and then nodded, apparently satisfied. 'Camera?' The word brought an instant silence to everyone and then Blake sat down, his hand pulling Nicola to the seat beside him. 'Action!'

The command brought a quick thrill to Nicola and she leaned forward in her seat. She had watched the cameras being prepared, watched the make-up artists darting forward at the last minute to add finishing touches to their work and now she was about to see the whole thing come together. She hadn't understood anything that Blake had made her write, but it didn't matter. A film was being made and she was part of it.

'You'll allow me to watch, I hope?' Blake snapped caustically and she shrank back, aware that she had been partially obscuring his view.

'I—I'm sorry,' she whispered and he gave a short, hard laugh.

'So you keep telling me,' he murmured coldly, his eyes on the action and, once again, she knew exactly the moment when his mind shut her out.

Nicola's tasks became part of a ritual and she was rarely more than a few feet from Blake each day. It was only when the filming was over every evening and the crew packed up their equipment that she was alone. She went back to the hotel each night but Blake stayed, the trailer his home.

That was how she got to know the others. Meeting them at dinner, mixing with them each day, it was impossible to remain apart, in spite of Blake's threats. The leading man was a rather aloof character who did nothing more than nod to her politely when they met, but he was the exception; several of the younger actors took an interest in her, one in particular.

'Watch Martin Cole,' Janet said to her quietly one evening when Nicola had been the centre of attraction for most of the time. 'The others are harmless, but he isn't.'

'He's just being friendly,' Nicola assured her. 'I can take care of myself, in any case.'

'Blake doesn't seem to think so from what I've seen,' Janet murmured with a long look at Nicola's slightly flustered face. 'If he knows that Martin is taking an interest, there'll be trouble.'

'I suppose he asked you to keep an eye on me?' Nicola surmised rather impatiently. 'I'm not an idiot.'

'He didn't ask me, as a matter of fact,' Janet murmured. 'I decided all by myself.'

'Why?' Nicola turned to her and asked the question with a sort of dread, wondering if she would say that as Blake's future wife it was her duty. She said no such thing.

'Who knows, darling? Because you're English? Because you've been ill? Probably, though, because if you get yourself into a fix Blake will take Martin apart, smash up the hotel and ditch the film. It's a sort of self-preservation. We've nearly made it to the end.'

'Blake wouldn't do that,' Nicola assured her with a tremulous smile. 'He would just take it out on me.'

'I doubt it.' Janet eyed her sceptically and then laughed. 'He might leave the film intact, but as to the rest, I can guarantee it, so, as I said, watch Martin.'

Nicola felt very much on edge after that and spent the rest of the evening with Janet, liking her more all the time. It was because of this newly acquired intimacy that she felt able to mutter her thoughts to Janet one day later when there was a slight break in the filming.

'Dorettc Ingham is very beautiful,' she mentioned as the actress in question, a very beautiful girl with ash-blonde hair, was almost falling all over Blake.

'Oh, yes,' Janet murmured wryly. 'She's making quite sure that Blake knows it, too. Have you noticed?'

'He—he doesn't seem to mind,' Nicola muttered, ashamed of herself for her miserable thoughts. Dorette Ingham was always with Blake and it was obvious that he enjoyed her adulation. He never snapped at her as he did at the others.

'Oh, Nicola!' Janet laughed. 'You don't know much about the film world and even less about how Blake works. Dorette has two more scenes before her part in the film is over. Watch Blake then. At the moment he's coaxing her along. I rather think she's expecting to get close to him. It's quite pitiful really and so stupid. She's good, you know. She doesn't need any of this starlet vamp attitude. It's going to be a long way to fall when Blake looks at her as if he's never seen her before, and he will do. I've seen it over and over. To Blake, the film is the only thing that matters.'

'You're close to him,' Nicola said, regretting her observation the moment the words had passed her lips.

'I've known him a long time,' Janet assured her comfortably. 'Blake and I go back a long way. It gives me special privileges.'

'Why don't you get a rest, Janet?' Blake asked quite tightly, coming up at that moment. 'Your big scene comes immediately after lunch, if the light holds like this,' he added, squinting up at the blue sky.

'Good idea,' Janet decided willingly. 'I could do with a rest.'

'You can stand down too,' Blake told Nicola, looking at her coolly. Since the day at the trailer he had almost ignored her and, sometimes, she felt close to tears. 'I won't need you until later,' he finished acidly when she just gazed at him a little forlornly. 'I have to spend some time with Dorette.'

Nicola nodded and turned away and she didn't get far before Dorette was there, smiling and charming, clinging to Blake's arm. Whatever Janet thought, it seemed to Nicola that Blake liked the attention, and she wandered off towards the old church, not really thinking about where she was going.

Here and there, people were doing a little private re-hearsing and nobody at all was paying attention to her. It was clear that this slight break was for Dorette's ben-efit, but everyone was making the most of it. She hadn't missed the way that Blake had cut her out away from Janet, either. It all added to her gloom.

The church was quite fascinating and Nicola climbed the steep steps, slipping inside through the partly opened door and wandering around. It was very old with an atmosphere of its own in spite of the presence of a film crew and actors. They were transitory, but this had stood here for a very long time, long before the old miners came.

She walked out through an archway at the side, a place where the wall was crumbling and the door had gone altogether. Above her the sky was blue, high clouds drifting along and she stepped forward, looking up to the one remaining tower, her face turning towards the church.

'*Nicky*!'

The sound of Blake's voice startled her, especially as he had called her that. Nobody had ever called her that and she turned her head in astonishment, amazed at the violence in his voice when he had not more than a few minutes ago told her she could do as she liked for a while.

'Don't move! Stand still!' He seemed to be frozen to the spot and his attitude did exactly the same to Nicola. She didn't know why, but suddenly she was frightened, even more frightened when she noticed everyone else standing like rock, staring up at her.

'Keep still!' Blake was already moving as he shouted again and she was rigid with shock as she saw him start to run towards her, moving like the wind, tearing up the steps of the church. She looked down then, her eyes free of him as he went momentarily out of sight at the top of the steps. It was the last thing she should have done because then she knew why Blake had roared at her, then she knew why he had told her to stand still.

She had stepped back to look up at the church and she had stepped to the very edge of a long drop, not only a drop the height of the steps, but a long fall to the ground that was worse. The church had been built on a hill and now most of the hill had been eroded by the weather and the salt air of the tides. One more step and she would have fallen, and it was not a fall that anyone could have survived.

Nicola started to tremble, too scared to move. All she had to do was step forward, but her legs refused to help her and she was still there, her eyes terrified, her hands shaking as Blake raced through the church and reached for her, gathering her to him and pulling her to safety.

He said nothing at all and Nicola was incapable of words. Blake lifted her into his arms and walked out of the church and down the steps, holding her against his chest, ignoring everyone who came to console her.

'Blake?' Janet appeared, obviously having heard him shout, but he ignored Janet too.

'I—I can walk,' Nicola stammered, but Blake never stopped. His arms were like steel and he went straight to his trailer, opening the door and stepping inside with his burden. Then he put her down and turned to slam the door shut, almost in the face of Dorette Ingham, who obviously did not yet know his savage ways.

He stood quite still, his lean, powerful body held tightly as if he were holding in a murderous rage and Nicola had no alternative but to face him.

'Blake,' she began shakily. 'I—I...'

She got no further because Blake simply exploded with fury. He grasped her slender shoulders, hauling her against the hard wall of his chest, his eyes blazing down at her, pinning her fast like a butterfly.

'You stupid, idiotic, incompetent *pest!*'

He just roared the words at her and then let her go, walking out and slamming the door behind him with enough violence to make the whole trailer shudder.

Nicola was shuddering too. She sank to the nearest seat, her hands covering her face as she tried to come to terms with her trembling, with Blake's wild anger and with her own foolish actions. She had never behaved idiotically in her life. She was methodical, careful, competent. Now, though, she could well understand why Blake thought she was none of those things. She was so obsessed with him that she seemed to have no control over her own mind.

He had to be faced and the sooner the better. She glanced at herself in the mirror and then went outside. Everything was normal, as normal as anything could be with a raging tiger at large. He was back with Dorette, walking through her scene with her, and it gave some of the others time to glance at her sympathetically. They had heard Blake's opinion of her. He had roared so loudly that it must have been heard for miles, she surmised ruefully.

'Don't take it to heart, Nicola,' Martin Cole came up and grinned at her. 'We all get that from time to time, although we don't usually try to kill ourselves first. We do that *after* Blake has made his opinion known.'

'I deserved it,' Nicola murmured. She could see Blake approaching and she didn't want any more trouble.

'That's not what you deserve at all,' Martin said seductively. 'I can think of much better things.'

'Rehearse your scene with Dorette,' Blake snapped, arriving like Nemesis. He stood and stared at Nicola as Martin left rather hurriedly and then he very visibly relaxed. 'What the hell were you doing up there?' he asked more quietly than she had expected.

'I was just sort of wandering around,' she confessed. 'You didn't need me and I didn't know what to do so...'

'So you decided to kill yourself?' he enquired drily. 'I had thought you might make a coffee and have a rest. I even considered it possible that you might make one for me.'

'But I didn't know and, in any case, I couldn't. I mean there's nowhere I could...'

'You've forgotten the trailer, I see,' Blake murmured. 'What's mine is yours, or didn't you know that?'

Nicola just looked at him helplessly, tied into knots already and his hand came out unexpectedly and curved round her face.

'You want to make two coffees now?' he asked softly. 'After that fright I feel as if I could do with at least half a cup of brandy in mine.'

'Why did you call me that?' she asked, looking up at him and the eyes that were normally narrowed on her in irritation began to sparkle with laughter.

'Nicky?' he enquired. 'Two syllables, easier to shout.' He laughed down at her and then turned her quite gently to the trailer. 'The coffee?' he murmured.

All the time she was getting it ready, Nicola was asking herself why she had got off so lightly. As far as she could see, he had been angry with her all the week for doing much less than she had done today. She gave a rather tragic sigh and went out, carefully carrying two mugs of hot coffee and, already, the next scene was being filmed, a hush over everything and Blake's eyes dark and intent on the production.

He was sitting and someone had moved her chair. There wasn't much chance of Blake yelling for one now and she handed him his drink, getting no acknowledgement whatever, and then sat cross-legged on the ground by his feet. It was still very fascinating to her and, as she sipped her hot drink, Nicola admiringly watched Janet in action. Even with the cameras around, the make-up artist and everyone else standing just out of range, Janet seemed to make it all real.

'Cut!' Blake shouted, standing to make his presence felt even more. 'It looks wrong as you move down the steps. Try it again, Janet.'

Everyone waited as the part was rehearsed and Blake was still not satisfied. Nicola reckoned that Janet had been up and down those steps at least five times in the end and, even from her position, she could see the beginnings of distress on her face.

'Blake,' she said quietly, taking her courage firmly into her hands. 'This is hurting Janet. That leg is still not too comfortable.'

'Damn! I forgot!' He stood again and shouted across. 'OK, move on to the next part. We'll do the steps tomorrow.' Janet visibly relaxed. There was a flurry of movement, silence and then Blake called, 'Action!' before sinking back to his seat.

Nicola was just congratulating herself on getting away with telling him he was wrong when his hand came to her head, his fingers gently ruffling her hair.

'Thanks, sweetheart,' he said softly.

He said nothing else, but for a few seconds his hand stayed on her hair, absently stroking it and Nicola was glad he couldn't see her face; she was glowing with happiness. What Blake did meant so much to her and she had never imagined he would ever be gentle. She just sat as still as a mouse, watching the remainder of the filming, telling herself quite firmly that she could not, in any circumstances, rest back against Blake's leg, although she wanted to very much.

'I'm sorry about the steps, Janet,' Blake said when the scene was over and Janet came across. 'I totally forgot. Nicola called me to order, though.'

'A friend in the enemy camp,' Janet said, smiling down at Nicola who still sat by Blake. 'The leg was giving me some pain. A few more times and I would have screamed.'

'I know just what you mean,' Blake muttered as Dorette came swaying across to them. 'I often feel like that myself.'

Janet shot a look of amusement at Nicola and then escaped while Blake stood, reached down and pulled Nicola to her feet.

'I always wanted a slave to sit obediently by me,' he said quietly. 'I've never been able to afford one until now.' His hands were on her shoulders and, as Nicola looked up at him, her cheeks wildly flushed, his lips tilted in a wry smile. 'Close your eyes, honey,' he murmured. 'You're doing it again.' Nicola escaped, too. Blake might be simply coaxing Dorette along but, all the same, she couldn't stay there and watch. In any case, as far as she could see, she had been dismissed.

Whatever Blake's thoughts, he never got the chance to speak to her until they were almost ready to leave and then he took her arm, turning her away from the others and walking with her until they were far enough away to be private.

'No telephone call?' he asked and Nicola shook her head, ashamed to realise that she had forgotten all about it in her desire to be with Blake.

'I would have told you.'

'Sure.' He let go of her arm and walked along with his hands in his pockets, a frown on his face. 'We've got two more days here and then it's all over. The camp then becomes home, any messages sent there.' He turned and looked down at her, quite obviously thinking deeply. 'Get the bus,' he said after a second. 'I have a few things to do. I'll eat at the hotel tonight and then I can phone Dr Gregory. If there's no news, I'll tell him we're almost wrapped up here.'

'You—you don't have to be in this, Blake,' Nicola pointed out quietly, looking up at him and his frown deepened for a second.

'I am in it,' he reminded her. 'I was in it from the moment I knew about you.' She just nodded and went to the bus. He was in it whether he liked it or not, actually, because Aunt Mary had to be shielded and Blake had taken it upon himself to change her own future.

'Had your secret little chat?' Martin Cole asked suggestively as Nicola climbed on board and the bus set off.

'We had family things to discuss,' Nicola managed skilfully, well aware that everyone was listening. 'Blake is—is almost my cousin.'

'He's almost my hero, but he wouldn't go white to the lips if I stood at the edge of a drop,' Martin drawled, and Janet cut in sharply as Nicola looked a bit embarrassed.

'No. He'd trip you neatly and shout "Action".'

There was a roar of laughter in which Martin joined readily and Nicola glanced gratefully at Janet before sliding into the next seat.

'Thanks,' she murmured and Janet smiled wryly.

'Just paying you back for this afternoon's rescue. Blake doesn't usually leave himself open for speculation,' she added thoughtfully. 'I must say that I was as intrigued as everyone else. I'm just too cunning to say anything.'

There was an odd sound to her voice and Nicola's heart sank. She knew the tone of jealousy when she heard it and it reminded her all over again that, in all probability, Janet and Blake were more than friends. As Janet had said, they went back a long way. Why she was anxious about Dorette when there was somebody as charming, talented and sophisticated as Janet Browning around, she didn't know.

CHAPTER NINE

THE evening became a party and nobody knew exactly why, although there was speculation that Martin had engineered it. Right from the first there was merriment, and when Blake walked in unexpectedly, joining them for dinner, there were a few worried looks.

'Relax,' Blake said ironically. 'There's tomorrow and the day after and then we've finished here. As tomorrow is mainly Janet and Bruce, a few bleary eyes won't be noticed.'

'Those steps again,' Janet said with a wry look at Blake and he grinned at her.

'I'll lower my standards. I don't want Nicola chastising me again.' His remark brought a quick silence and a few further speculative looks, but Blake was in one of his moods to charm and, as they were greatly relieved not to have been reprimanded, nobody said anything on the subject of Nicola and her correcting of Blake.

After dinner he disappeared and Nicola was on edge, knowing he had gone to phone England. When he came back he was frowning, not that anyone else noticed. The party spirit had gripped most of them and it was only Nicola who stood watching him worriedly.

'Nothing yet,' he muttered, taking her arm and leading her to the bar. 'I suppose it's too early to expect anything. We should be back there on the spot.' He sounded so much in earnest about that and Nicola was quite startled to realise how much he was prepared to crowd into his busy life in order to get to the bottom of her own particular problems.

147

'Aunt Mary will probably never know anything about it,' she said quietly. 'You can't take on everything, Blake. You're too busy, and why should you anyway? Aunt Mary need never find out because, sooner or later, I'll be gone.'

'Later than later,' he murmured, tightening his hand on her arm. 'Don't talk about leaving. It merely infuriates me.'

'Are you going to dance with me, Blake?' Dorette appeared in a glittering dress and stood in front of them, and Nicola soon knew what Janet had meant.

'Not if I can help it,' he murmured cuttingly as he steered Nicola away. Dorette looked utterly stunned and, at the other end of the bar, Janet caught Nicola's eyes and raised her glass mockingly. Dorette's part in the film was finished. Blake's patience had run out.

'When we get back,' Blake murmured, as if nothing had happened to interrupt their conversation, 'you'll have to field the calls. I'll fix it with Mary so that it doesn't look suspicious.'

'Won't you be there?' Nicola spun round to look up at him, but his eyes were on Janet and he was smiling.

'One day only,' he said quietly, never even looking at her. 'I have things to do.' Janet moved across to them as if he had called her and Nicola knew that he had completely forgotten about her. She knew what he had to do. Now that the film was finished, he and Janet would be going away together.

'Want to try this dance?' Janet asked in a throaty voice, and Blake smiled down at her.

'What about the leg?'

'You'll hold me up, as usual.' Janet looked up at him and he just led her away without a backward glance, leaving Nicola with her drink and no company at all. It was so very obvious, the couple understood each other perfectly, even to the extent that Blake would use his masculine charm on Dorette when it was necessary. Nicola felt what she was, an outsider, someone who had come into Blake's powerful life because he cared about Mary. She had never felt quite so empty inside, so alone.

It didn't last long because Martin Cole was right there, very eager to take Blake's place, and Nicola was so hurt, so humiliated that she threw caution to the winds and encouraged him. She made a great effort, desperate that Blake should not see her hurt, stifling the urgent voice inside that tried to tell her how much Blake had come to mean to her.

After that she avoided Blake. He finally looked round for her, a feeling of duty no doubt as he had brought her here and away from her aunt, but Nicola had no intention of letting him know how she felt. She moved away when he seemed to be about to speak to her, laughing gaily into Martin's eyes and giving the impression that she was enjoying herself and basking in the attention she was getting.

It was not long before Blake became thunderous-looking, but Janet was always there and the sight of them together drove Nicola even further. It was hot, the doors and windows thrown open to the cooler night air and, when Martin brought her a drink, Nicola was grateful; so grateful, in fact, that she never considered the alcohol content. After a while, and after several more drinks, she was decidedly light-headed, no longer sufficiently in touch with the world to feel pain when she saw Blake. She was becoming anaesthetised to everything, otherwise she would have seen the satisfied look in Martin's eyes.

What she did see, finally, was the look on Blake's face as he cut in ruthlessly as she danced, yet again, with Martin. He took her into his arms and held her fast, glaring down at her, and she was so far gone that she giggled.

'Why, Blake! Have you lost Janet?'

She was bubbling with laughter, couldn't seem to stop, and Blake simply turned and walked her to the door, his arm tightly around her waist, the pressure hurting her.

They were outside and heading for his car before she managed to get any words out, and then she complained loudly. 'You're hurting me!'

'Not as much as I'd like to!' he bit out savagely. 'If you're going to keel over, you can do it in private.'

'I am not going to keel over,' Nicola assured him in a dignified voice, a voice slightly spoiled as she giggled again. 'I was enjoying myself at the party and Martin will be looking for me.'

'Not if he values his pretty face!' Blake rasped, forcing her into the car. 'Right at this moment, his knees are knocking together—I can assure you of that!'

He took off at an alarming speed and Nicola gripped the door of the open-topped car frantically.

'Where are you taking me?' she asked sharply. 'Take me back at once!'

'When you're sober,' he growled. 'Until then, you're with me. If Cole wants a long, exciting night, he can spend it with Dorette.'

'He never even considered . . .' Nicola began in an outraged voice, getting the meaning of his nasty remarks even though her head was swimming.

'Of course he never considered it,' Blake grated, shooting her a look of fury. 'He planned it. All he needed was an idiot—and you're ready-made!'

Nicola never answered because everything was becoming hazy, the road almost dancing in front of her eyes and, when Blake drew up with a great squealing of tyres outside his trailer, she couldn't even get out of the car.

Not that she was allowed to linger. Blake reached inside and hauled her out unceremoniously, almost dragging her inside. It was dark, no lights on at all, and Nicola stood exactly where he had put her, a quick flare of fear prickling her skin.

'It's dark,' she whispered shakily and she heard Blake's harsh laugh.

'It would have been more than dark in Cole's room. Think what you're missing.'

'You don't think that I...? Blake! Put some lights on!' There was the sound of panic in Nicola's voice and Blake flicked on the lights and looked at her with angry satisfaction.

'The trouble with you is that you don't know what to be scared of,' he grated, 'and there are plenty of ways to be frightened out of your wits. After the episode of the church and now Cole, I'm beginning to think that you're trying them all out.'

Nicola sank to the nearest seat, her head in her hands. It felt like somebody else's head and she gave a soft little moan.

'I feel terrible. You'll have to take me back. I've got to go to bed.'

'So you have,' Blake snapped, 'and this is where you're doing it! If there's to be any wandering in the night it's not going to be by Martin Cole. If you have to put up a fight, you can fight the pillow. You sleep here. I'll bunk down on the couch.'

He pulled her to her feet none too gently and Nicola found herself being hustled into the room at the end that was partitioned off into a small but comfortable bedroom. The thought of staying here with Blake only vaguely entered her mind. All she could see was the bed, the inviting comfort of it, somewhere to rest her aching head, and she sank towards it immediately.

'Not so fast!' Blake growled, pulling her back. 'You'll be enough of a wreck in the morning without having slept in your clothes.'

Before she could stop him, the zip of her dress was plunged down and Nicola raised panic-stricken eyes as Blake slid her dress away in one swift movement and lifted her out of it as it fell to the floor.

'Blake!' Her alarm did nothing to ease his temper and he glared at her, ignoring that fact that she stood swaying in front of him in her slip and very little else. He walked out and was back almost immediately with a dark pyjama top which he thrust into her hands.

'Put this on,' he ordered angrily. 'If you can sleep off the unaccustomed liquid refreshment before the others stir, I'll take you back to get changed at first light.'

He walked out and slammed the door and Nicola struggled out of her slip and into the jacket of his pyjamas. Then she fell into bed. At the moment she felt too queasy to be ashamed of herself, but later the shame would come. She had never behaved badly in her life, but now she seemed to be catching up fast.

As for Martin Cole and his intentions, she had been too jealous to see danger. She gave a shudder and snuggled down with a moan of pain as her head began to throb again. At least she was safe, no matter how angry Blake was. Within seconds she was asleep, not even bothering to put out the light.

In the middle of the night, Nicola awoke with a devastating thirst and she knew it was useless to try to go back to sleep. The thought of where she was seemed to be unimportant; the only real thing on her mind was getting to some source of water and she was glad that the light was still on, otherwise she would have been disorientated. As it was, she knew exactly where she had been sleeping and she also knew where the fridge was.

She crept out of the room and made her way towards the kitchen area at the end. The lights were out in the rest of the trailer, but with the light from the bedroom she could see reasonably well. She could also see Blake, stretched out on the couch and fast asleep. Normally she would have wanted to stand and simply look at him. The sheet was pushed down to his waist, the strong muscles of his chest relaxed in sleep, and she gave a little shaken sigh as she looked quickly away.

She moved past him on silent feet, hardly daring to breathe and, as she passed, his hand shot out and captured her wrist, making her jump and gasp with shock.

'What are you up to now?' he asked in a sleepily intrigued voice.

'I'm terribly thirsty,' Nicola confessed, almost in a whisper. She was now embarrassingly aware that she was standing there in the jacket of his pyjamas, a long length of leg showing below it.

'Ah! The demon drink,' Blake murmured. His hand was still tightly around her wrist and she looked down at him worriedly, so worriedly in fact that he suddenly grimaced and let her go. 'There's iced water in the fridge. I'll not offer to assist you. You're wearing my pyjamas; my putting on the remaining half seemed pretty pointless.'

Nicola's face flushed and she was glad to turn away and help herself to the water, too thirsty even to wait for a drink until she got it back to her bed. She drank greedily and then filled up the glass again before making her way back.

'Better?' Blake was still watching her and she avoided his eyes.

'Yes, thank you.' She moved as quickly as she could, but he caught her hand again as she passed and stopped her flight.

'How's the head?' he asked wryly and she looked down at him quickly, expecting caustic comments.

'It's all right. There's only this thirsty feeling.'

'Then you escaped lightly,' Blake murmured, releasing her hand again. 'All we have to do now is get you a change of clothes and manage a cool and dignified look in the morning.'

'What will everybody think?' Nicola muttered and he turned on his side, closing his eyes, a slight smile edging his lips.

'Who knows? Who cares for that matter? Goodnight, honey.'

His eyes were firmly closed and he was also tired of the conversation.

Nicola hurried back to bed and closed the door between them. It didn't seem to matter very much now that he had been furious with her the night before. He didn't care at all what people thought, but then he never had done. Mulling it over, she supposed he called plenty of women honey, if he was in a good mood. Did he also call them sweetheart? She had never had the chance to see how Janet had reacted to their rather dramatic departure. She would not have liked it at all, though.

Nicola closed her eyes and tried not to think too deeply about it. Two more days and this would all be over. She had not been deceived by Blake's words at the hotel. She would have to take all the calls when they got back because he would be going away and she knew he would be going away with Janet. She had seen it in his eyes. That was why she had behaved so stupidly with Martin Cole.

In spite of her thirst and her miserable thoughts, Nicola slept immediately, and she was still deeply asleep when Blake came in to wake her up.

'Nicola!' He shook her gently and she opened her eyes, quite surprised to see him there, until she remembered. 'It's already five,' he told her. 'I intended to get you up before this and take you back to change. I slept too late, though, and now we'll really have to hustle. Otherwise, they'll be here and you'll be wearing your party dress all day.'

He looked as if he had just hurried out of bed himself. He was in jeans but so far he had not put a shirt on, and Nicola felt a burst of guilt that she had landed him in this situation.

'I'll get dressed quickly,' she promised. 'I'm sorry you got involved in this.'

'It's not worrying me any,' he said quietly. He sat on the edge of the bed, looking into her upturned face, and all the feelings she had bottled up inside began to grow again as she looked into the dark eyes. 'How do you feel?' he asked and she gave a rueful smile.

'Fine. Better than I deserve to feel. Making a fool of myself is one thing, dragging you into it is another entirely.'

'I don't remember being dragged. I do remember exploding on to the charming scene.' He was watching her closely and Nicola looked up at him with a certain amount of pleading, her eyes searching his face.

'It was more stupid than charming,' she confessed huskily. 'I don't know why I did it.'

'That's all right,' Blake assured her softly, his eyes holding hers. 'I know why you did it. That being the case, I'm inclined to let you off lightly—now that I've regained my temper.'

She just looked up at him warily, hoping he did not know why she had gone so readily to Martin, but he stared down at her and there was no escaping his probing look. His eyes moved over her face and she saw the smile die away slowly, a taut look coming to take its place.

'Golden hair and green eyes,' he murmured, almost to himself. His hand came to her cheek and stroked slowly over the silken skin. 'You even look good in the early morning after a shattering evening.'

Nicola just went on looking at him, her eyes doing what they always did, roaming over his face with a longing she didn't even know was there. Her gaze slid almost secretly to his smooth wide shoulders, to his powerful chest. There was a scattering of dark hair across it, masculine, strong and inviting her touch. She took a small shaky breath as her eyes went slowly back to his face and his hand slid around the back of her neck, tightening almost painfully.

'God! Don't look at me like that!' he muttered unevenly.

But she couldn't help looking at him, her cheeks flushed softly and her eyes stared at him helplessly as he looked down at her, colour along his own cheekbones too.

'Nicola, don't!' he said harshly. 'I didn't bring you here for this. I brought you here to protect you.'

'You—you do protect me,' she whispered. She moistened her lips, her tongue running along them anxiously and his dark eyes followed the movement intently as he took a great shuddering breath.

'I can't—not now.' His voice was heavy and deep and his gaze left her lips reluctantly. 'I'm not even sure which one of us needs protecting at this moment.'

His head bent to hers and she never closed her eyes. She wanted to see him until the last second, to watch him come closer, to feel the moment when he would kiss her. His eyes never left her either; they were intent on her lips and then his arms slid round her, tightening and arching her from the pillows as his mouth crushed hers.

Nicola's arms went around him instantly, her hands running along his tanned shoulders, feeling the masculine smoothness of his skin. She wanted to kick the sheets aside, to be even closer to him, and he acted as if he could hear her thoughts. His mouth never left its devastating onslaught on hers, but his hand grasped the sheet and pulled it aside as he came down beside her and crushed her against him.

There were no words. There was just a fire between them that was growing by the second, the only noise the harsh, uneven sound of their breathing. She had never been so close to him before and Nicola moved with a soft willingness as he pulled her closer, her hands moving over his face, a little moan of protest at the back of her throat that she could not entwine herself to him even more.

Blake held her against him as he slipped the few buttons of the jacket and then she heard a low sound of satisfaction deep in his throat as his hand moved possessively to her breast. She gave a sharp gasping cry as his lean fingers closed around the swollen mound and his kiss deepened as his thumb moved slowly across the sharp, excited nipple, the action sending a shaft of feeling down through her whole body.

He lifted his head, almost tearing his lips from hers, his eyes dark and burning as they looked down at her silken breast cradled in his palm.

'I want you!' he said harshly, 'I want you now!'

His lips captured the high throbbing peak and Nicola cried out in shock, her whole body leaping under his touch, and instantly he was gentle, his lips lifting to move comfortingly along her cheeks and neck.

'Oh, honey,' he murmured thickly. 'I won't hurt you.' He sank down beside her, the tremendous sexual tension easing from his body. 'Come here,' he whispered. 'Let me touch you, Nicky.'

She was more than willing, the moment of panic passing as if it had never been, and her instant submission brought forth a low sound of masculine satisfaction from Blake. He eased the jacket from her and tossed it aside, his hand moving over her seductively as he held her and looked down at her.

'Is this what you've been waiting for, sweetheart?' he asked huskily as his lips trailed over her shoulders and moved down to find her breast gently. 'Is this why you look at me like that?'

Nicola murmured desperately against his skin and he drew back to look at her, his face taut and sensuous as he saw her dazed eyes, her wildly flushed cheeks. His dark eyes were intent on her face as his fingers teased the rosebud of her nipple and she gasped with pleasure, a pleasure so great that she could not keep still. She melted against him, her mouth open against his skin, and Blake's hand moved down her slender flanks to ease away her last remaining garment.

'Do you want me to love you, Nicky?' he asked thickly, but she could not answer. His hands were setting her on fire and her only sound was a fretful murmur of demand that made Blake crush her beneath him. Her arms were tightly around his neck, her body straining against his and Blake's hands went to his belt with an urgency that she could not miss.

'Nicola!' he groaned in a shaken voice as she eagerly began to help him. Neither of them could keep still, their bodies arching together, both of them impatient to be closer, and then they both heard the sound of an engine; the unmistakable noise of the bus pulling on to the level ground not far away. It was time for the cast to be brought, time for the crew. She was lying naked in Blake's arms and, outside, everyone had arrived.

Blake went on holding her and they stared into each other's eyes as if a dream was receding. Blake's hands tightened on her, his long fingers flexing and, even then, she couldn't help the way she simply submitted, her actions decided by her body, her mind not her own.

His hand moved to her face, gripping it fast, almost hurting her, and his eyes had never been so dark, so intent.

'If I thought they'd just go away,' he said thickly, 'I wouldn't move.' His fingers tightened in her hair, his breathing still erratic. 'I want you, but I want you too much to take you in a hurry.'

He got up, refastening his belt as he looked down at her and she was astonished that she felt no shame, even when his eyes moved over her hotly.

'What will I do?' she whispered, her eyes clinging to his.

'My inclination is to tell you to stay right where you are,' he murmured, his face still taut with desire. 'My common sense urges me to tell you to get dressed.'

'But what shall I wear?' Nicola asked, bewildered by the heat that still flooded through her limbs. It brought a smile to his face and he relaxed almost at once.

'Well, the pyjama jacket was fascinating,' he pondered, 'but it's not really right for the occasion.' He suddenly reached across and touched her face. 'Get dressed and I'll tell the driver to take you back to the hotel.'

'Oh, but...!'

'He can bring you back straight away,' Blake added when she looked dismayed 'You can then get me something to eat. By the time you get back, things will be moving. Right now, I've got to go. Take your time. I'll hand out orders to the driver.'

He walked out and then came back

'Got the nerve to face a few questioning looks?' he enquired, and Nicola looked up at him, her face still flushed and dazed.

'Yes. I don't really care.' She didn't. All she cared about was Blake. She loved him with a sort of desperation that she knew was dangerous and asking for heartache. It was there, though, and nothing was going to change that, even if it was to be nothing but this time here, nothing but his heated kisses.

'You never fail to astonish me,' he said softly. 'You're innocence is blindingly obvious and you never protect yourself. You see only what you wish to see.'

He walked out, leaving her to struggle into her clothes and try to improve her appearance, but nothing would wipe the look from her eyes, she knew that without any doubt. It was the look that Blake had seen, the look he had warned her about before. This time he had been ready to take everything she offered and she could hardly blame him.

She managed to slide out while there was the normal amount of morning chaos and she ignored the way the driver glanced at her. It was none of his business. It was nobody's business except hers and Blake's.

'Going for your breakfast now?' the driver enquired drily as he stopped outside the hotel.

'No. I'm going straight back. I expect you've been told to wait for me?' Nicola said sharply. 'Give me fifteen minutes.' She assumed it wasn't the first time he had made this sort of run, working as he did in films, but the thought that he might have made this sort of run for Blake, the thought that he might have brought some other woman back to some other hotel, drove into her heart like a knife. It made her hurry, made her feel icy cold, and when she finally got back to the location she was as controlled as she was going to be, ready to meet any eyes, providing they were not Blake's.

She never went to him, she just went to the trailer and made coffee and toast for Blake, tea and toast for herself and then she took it out to him with a cool look on her face that kept any interested looks at a distance. She wasn't flushed and starry-eyed and she almost smiled when the looks she got were deeply puzzled.

Blake took his breakfast without a word and later she removed the plates and mugs and put them back in the trailer, staying a minute to wash them up. After that she was ready for work and she sat beside Blake as if nothing had happened. Whenever she got the chance, she moved away from him, and she was relieved to find that this morning Janet was working hard, her big scene acted out for the cameras. It took everyone's attention, too, including Blake's, and gradually the frantic heat she had felt in his arms died away. When she glanced at his face, he was working—there was no other way to describe it.

At lunchtime he was strictly busy with Janet and Bruce, eating his lunch on the move and hammering out details with them, forcing them through last-minute rehearsals with the same old ruthlessness until Nicola felt that she had imagined his desperation this morning. She couldn't believe that the powerful man with hard, narrowed eyes was the same being who had held her and caressed her frantically, his body wildly aroused over her own.

She kept up her own personal charade until midafternoon and then Blake signalled for her, handing her the notebook as she sank down in the seat beside him.

'What shall I write?' she asked, managing to keep her voice businesslike.

'Nothing!' he grated. 'Just be near me. Keep this up and I'll give them all a real lesson in romance, right here with you.'

A shiver passed over her skin and she looked hastily away from his angry eyes.

'Blake,' she began anxiously, but he never let her finish.

'What do you expect but savagery when you get involved with a savage?' he growled. His mind went back to business and Nicola sat like a mouse, almost afraid to breathe until he gave a ragged sigh and relaxed. His hand came to her nape, moving under the heavy fall of hair, his fingers soothing and coaxing against her skin until she too relaxed, a pained excitement racing through her.

When she looked up, his eyes were on her and not on the production at all. The dark gaze was running over the swollen evidence of her breasts, tight against her sweater.

'OK,' he said softly, his eyes moving to hers. 'I forgive you.' He looked at her for far too long and Nicola flushed.

'Shouldn't you be—be watching the action?' she whispered.

'Oh, I'll see the rushes,' he murmured sardonically. His eyes went back to the cameras and the actors, but the tiger grin was back in place and Nicola took a long time to calm down. As to her newly acquired coolness, she had lost it.

When everything was being packed up for the evening she felt a rush of anxiety. What would Blake say? What would he expect of her? She was shy with him again, appalled at her own actions this morning. She tried to avoid him, but he found her easily.

'That's it, then,' he stated emphatically and her heart missed a beat, her eyes meeting his with panic lurking in their depths. She just dared not ask what he meant and, after looking down at her for a second, he told her.

'We've finished,' he said quietly. 'We managed it all today. Tomorrow we go home.'

And then he would be away soon, away with Janet. Nicola had no doubt at all about that and she looked down quickly, avoiding his eyes. Not knowing what to say.

'Surely you're glad?' he goaded softly. 'Surely you admire the swift efficiency. In spite of all the setbacks, we're right on schedule, not a penny wasted.'

'Very good,' Nicola managed. 'You—you must be very pleased.'

Blake began to laugh, a dark low laugh that had her looking up quickly, her wide green eyes caught and held fast by the deep brown of his.

'Tomorrow I'll collect you straight after breakfast,' he told her in an amused voice. 'Don't panic, Nicola. Tonight you sleep at the hotel. That should puzzle them.' She just nodded and, as someone called to him, Blake walked off and left her.

He did not come up to the hotel that evening and, as soon as she could, Nicola escaped to bed. There had been no comments about her night away with Blake. Everyone kept strictly to film talk and Martin Cole stayed well away from her.

There was no sign of Janet and, when somebody asked where she was Martin had his chance.

'She already left,' he stated, with a glance at Nicola. 'She has other things to do. I don't think she's driving far.'

There was an uncomfortable silence before everyone started talking at once and Nicola did not have to have things spelled out for her. Janet was with Blake. She would probably have been with him the night before if events had not forced Blake to leave early and have a guest for the night. As to what had happened this morning, Nicola knew she had provoked him beyond reason.

The fact that he arrived for her the next morning with no sign of Janet in tow meant nothing. Janet would now be on her way. Blake had simply come to collect his liability. He had called her that jokingly, but she felt it very deeply now. She had no right to be here, no right to sit beside him in the car as he pulled away from the hotel and made for the main highway. The fact that he had forced her to come to California and had almost forced her to be here with him, never entered her mind. She was a very unwilling burden, but she was a burden all the same.

Blake was silent, saying almost nothing for the whole of the drive. When they stopped for something to eat he seemed to be grimly wrapped in his thoughts and Nicola kept silent too. She was surprised and alarmed when, almost back to the house, Blake pulled off the road and stopped the car.

They were parked on a wide area, looking over the ocean and, for a moment, Blake said nothing at all. Nicola didn't dare. She watched the waves, her eyes following the breakers that crashed on the shore, the force of the water channelled into a small bay. The sun caught the white tops of the waves and the frothy end of their voyage as the energy was spilled on the rocky shoreline.

'What will you do when this mystery about your father is solved?' Blake asked quietly, his eyes also on the ocean.

'There's nothing to do,' Nicola said. 'He died. Whatever comes out, there's no getting away from that.'

'And if he died bravely, innocently, getting you out?'

'I keep telling myself that he did, that it was all some dreadful mix-up, that . . .' She couldn't go on, and for a moment Blake was silent at the choked sound of her voice.

'You'll go back?' he asked, after a while. He still looked out, away from her, his eyes on the changing pattern of the waves; Nicola felt the stillness in him, the waiting.

'Whatever happens, I'll go back,' she managed steadily, and he spun round to look at her then.

'You'll just go? Leave Mary?' The cold accusation hurt but she faced him.

'I live in England. I have a life there. It may not be as glamorous as your life, but it's there, all the same. I've met my aunt and I'm glad. I'm grateful to you.'

'A long time ago I told you I didn't need gratitude,' he rasped, staring at her angrily. 'Mary doesn't need it either. She needs you.'

'Don't blackmail me, Blake,' Nicola warned softly. 'Whatever you say, I'll go—and I'll go soon.' She had to go because she couldn't stay here, close to Blake. He should know that. Perhaps he thought she was like him, treating feelings with utter indifference. Even sitting here beside him was a torture and tears suddenly came to her eyes, making her turn her head away.

He was back to staring at the waves, silent and angry, and he did not know what was happening to her, how crushed she felt, how the tears were now flowing fast and silently until he turned his head and looked at her.

'Nicola!' He reached for her, pulling her into his arms even though she pushed against his strong chest and tried hard to escape. 'I didn't mean to make you cry,' he sighed against her hair when she at last stopped fighting him. 'I should never have taken you with me.'

'No,' Nicola agreed. 'You didn't need me.' He looked down at her steadily, his hand curving round her face.

'What do I need, after all?' he asked harshly. He bent his head, kissing her with a savage force that felt bruising and then he let her go, starting the car before she had even begun to recover. 'It's madness and you know it,' he rasped. 'You don't know me, you don't know how I live. I suspect that you don't even like me. You've discovered desire and you're letting it overwhelm you!'

He pulled back on to the road and the big car shot off with the same fury that seemed to be in Blake and, in any case, she had to agree. She didn't know Blake and she was overwhelmed. But it was love, not desire. Blake didn't understand about that. Love was something he would not feel, except perhaps the deep affection he had for Mary. He probably did not feel love for Janet, otherwise he would not have had to be reminded that she was hurting as she went up and down those steps. It was just that they knew each other, understood each other and were part of the same world.

'You're right,' she told him in an even voice. 'I don't like you very much, in spite of my gratitude. I've recovered from the madness, too. It's not overwhelming me now.'

It seemed for a minute that the car leapt forward even faster, but she did not look at Blake and he slowed to a more reasonable speed, his voice also controlled when he answered.

'Then stopping was a good idea. It cleared the air. Maybe you should go home, Nicola. We live in two different worlds.'

She knew that already and there was no need to answer, even if she had been able to summon up another lie.

CHAPTER TEN

WHEN Blake was called to the phone after dinner, Nicola tightened up inside. She went on talking blithely to her aunt, wondering how she was managing to speak at all, and he was a long time, so long, in fact, that she began to think he had just gone off and forgotten about her. When he did come back he kissed Mary on the cheek and said goodnight.

'I've got some work to do. I need Nicola too. We'll see you in the morning.'

It was all done smoothly and Mary had no suspicions, but Nicola followed him with her whole body held tensely. She had no idea what to expect and he went straight to his own private suite, motioning her inside and closing the door.

'Well, it's all solved,' he told her after walking around restlessly for a while. 'What do visitors say about England? Your policemen are wonderful?' He spun round to look at her, his tight expression relaxing as he saw her rather desperate face. 'Obviously you and Mary knew your father very well,' he said softly. 'He was a hero, after all. He just saved your life, Nicola, nothing more, nothing sinister or unlawful.'

Nicola reached for the settee and sat down, her legs weak and trembling.

'How do you know?' Her expression was an unhappy mixture of feelings. Nothing would bring her father back, but the pain that had come when she had thought he had carelessly ignored her safety was the lingering hurt.

'The police have arrested your father's partner, Benson. As it turned out, we never needed private investigators.'

'They said he had been checking the insurance,' Nicola told him, her eyes still on his face.

'I check mine from time to time. It's only sensible. He did nothing wrong, Nicola. All he did was love you enough to die for you.'

'I—I've always known that really,' she whispered. 'It was just the overwhelming evidence that so many people seemed to have.'

'And the fact that you were shocked, very ill when they forced the evidence on to you,' he stated grimly. 'You have nothing to reproach yourself with, nothing to regret because you could not at any time have altered the course of that particular destiny.'

'I know.' She felt very vulnerable, especially when Blake was watching her with sombre eyes and she stood and turned to the door. 'Thank you for—for finding out.'

'Wait!' Blake ordered quietly. 'I'd better tell you the rest. You're going to know sooner or later anyway and you'd better know from me. Benson was in over his head, living as if there was no tomorrow. Apart from material comforts which he never denied himself, he was running two homes with a woman in each. When the economic downturn hit the firm, he panicked. He started taking money out to bolster up his own private funds.'

Nicola sat down again, her eyes on Blake as he paced about the room. He glanced at her and then continued grimly,

'The night of the fire he was really in trouble because your father had taken the books home to study. Mistakenly, he told Benson that there were inexplicable discrepancies. Nothing has been proved yet, but it looks as if Benson started the fire with the hope of destroying the books. They think that it all got out of hand, that he never actually intended to burn the house down.'

Nicola winced at the memories and Blake came to sit beside her, taking her hand in his.

'In many ways, it was an accident,' he said, his eyes intent on her face. 'I didn't really want to tell you. It paints altogether too graphic a picture, but you'll know eventually and I might not be there to help then. I didn't want anyone else to tell you.'

Nicola nodded and looked down at their joined hands. It was a comfort that he cared enough to have thought of it, but nothing could erase the fact that her time with Blake was almost at an end.

'Did John Gregory tell you all this?' she asked, her eyes returning to his dynamic face.

'Yes. But I didn't want you to know. If there had been any way of keeping it from you I would have never told you. All you had to know was that your father loved you, that he never started the fire.'

'How do they know all this if the books were destroyed?'

'The company accountant had already seen the books. He was going to go over them again with your father that weekend. He didn't name any names, but he had his suspicions even with a brief inspection. Finally, he went to the police when the word got round that your father had started the fire himself. He just didn't believe it.'

Nicola stood, knowing that she had to get out of this room, to be by herself. Blake had said she could not have altered that destiny. She could not alter her present destiny either.

'I'm tired,' she said quietly. 'I'll go to bed.' She looked up at him, forcing herself to meet his dark eyes. 'Thank you. You didn't really need to do anything, but you've set my mind at rest, given me some peace.'

'Not much,' he pointed out in a harsh voice. 'The wheels were turning. You would have known before very long. In all probability I've taken more from you than I've given.'

'You haven't,' Nicola said simply. 'I could never have recovered without this new knowledge. Now I have to go back. Somebody has to see to the firm. At the moment there will be nobody who cares in charge.'

'You can't go yet!' Blake said fiercely, coming close to her. 'You'll be back where it all happened and you're not ready for it.'

'Maybe it will help me to get over things,' she murmured. Perhaps it would. Perhaps she would be too busy each day to think about Blake.

'I'll come with you!' He was assertive, possessive, but Nicola looked up at him and shook her head.

'No, Blake. I have to go alone. You've helped me enough and—and in any case...'

'What?' His hand cupped her face, forcing her to meet his eyes. 'In any case, what?'

'I have to get away from you. You said it would be best and you were right. It—it's been so unusual, not like me at all. I suppose I was a little vulnerable and a little dazzled by everything. I—I'm sorry I said I didn't like you. It wasn't true. I was just trying to hit back. But I'm recovered from the madness now, I don't feel overwhelmed any more.'

For a second Blake looked at her with blazing eyes, his hands tightly on her face, almost hurting.

'I say a lot of things during the course of a day,' he admitted harshly. 'I say plenty of things in a rage too. Don't throw them back at me because I never listen.'

'I'm only telling you that you were right,' Nicola whispered. 'You—you're more experienced and you knew. I don't feel anything now. I got over it.'

'Did you?' Blake growled. 'Then I'm just going to have to bring it back!'

He bent his head towards her as she held him off, wanting to keep her feelings hidden, but his arms lashed round her, crushing her to him, looking down at her when she stared up at him desperately.

'I don't want you to hold me, Blake,' she told him in a choked voice.

'Don't you, Nicola?' he asked harshly. 'Words are easy. I use them myself. In any case, I never believe anything you say, do I?'

Before she could answer, his mouth captured hers and Nicola was lost at once, her arms wound round his neck as she gave herself up to the deep and lingering kiss.

'Tell me you want to stay with me,' Blake murmured against her lips and all she could do was moan softly because the magic was back already, the heat enveloping her. 'Nicola!' he demanded against her lips and she knew that she was going down in the flames. She felt the swirling power of desire flooding through her, the need to be part of Blake.

But even in the haze of love she saw Janet's face, remembered the pain of seeing Blake with another woman. Even now when he was holding her, kissing her, he was planning to go away and stay with Janet. Blake was ruthless. He wanted her for now and he never lost in anything.

The thoughts chilled her and she went stiff in his arms, her head turning away as he pursued her.

'Nicky?' His hand curled round her face, forcing it back to him. 'You want me. Don't try to deny it.'

'I'm not trying to deny it,' she said in a tight little voice. 'I don't want you enough to stay here, though. I'm going home. Nothing you say or do will stop me. I'm not a mindless idiot. I have a career, another life, a country of my own and I'm going back.'

Blake let her go and she felt a wave of desolation sweep over her. For a second she wanted to deny everything she had said, to tell him that she would stay on any terms to be near him, but one look at his face was enough to stop anything like that. Blake had frozen over, his face was icy and the dark eyes that looked down at her were like black marble, lifeless as if his soul had fled.

'Tomorrow, I'm leaving for the cabin,' he said in a cold, controlled voice as he turned away from her. 'Before I go, I'll make all the arrangements for you.'

'There's no need——' she began, but he interrupted in his old, caustic manner, swinging round to stare at her as if she were a stranger.

'There's every need. I brought you here against your will. It's my duty to return you. Just give Mary a couple more days, that's all I ask. I'll have your flight arranged and I'll have you booked into an hotel in your home town.'

'Blake!' She wanted to be back in his arms, to tell him that she had been unhappily thinking of Janet, but the sight of his cold face stopped any words.

'When you leave,' he ordered, 'take all the clothes I brought you.'

'I can't do that...'

'You will!' he grated. 'Leave them here and I'll have Dolores burn them. I don't like memories.'

Nicola just murmured goodnight and left as quickly as she could. Now she would go back, now she would leave Blake, never see him again because she could not visit her aunt knowing that Blake would be here. It was his house. If he married Janet, then they would be living here.

She ran up the stairs and into her room, closing the door and leaning on it weakly. So many things had happened to her. One life had been destroyed and another had blossomed here with Blake. Now that too was ended. She had no real idea if she could put everything back together again. At the moment it was all too much. Tears began and she just let them flow, hoping that they would heal some of the wounds she felt. There was nobody to hear her cry and she just let her anguish pour out.

Next morning Blake had gone and when Nicola went down to breakfast, her aunt was sitting with a rather gloomy expression on her face.

'Blake left in the middle of the night,' she told Nicola miserably. 'He never even said goodbye. It's not like him at all. There was just a note on the table. Lots of times he's had to fly out in the night, but he's always come in to wake me to say goodbye. This time, nothing.'

Nicola felt guilty. She knew why he had gone like that. He had been too angry to see anyone. If he had come to see his stepmother he would have only upset her and he would never do that.

'The note said you were leaving, Nicola,' Mary continued. 'Blake says you have to go back.'

'Yes, I must,' Nicola said quietly. She sat down and looked at her aunt with all the affection she had come to feel. 'There's a lot you don't know. We—Blake and I kept it from you, but now I think you should know.'

'It's about your father,' Mary surmised. 'It's about Kevin?'

'Yes.' Nicola managed to smile and take her aunt's hand in her own. 'He was a very brave man, a wonderful man. You were quite right.'

Two days later, Nicola was ready to leave. Blake had arranged her ticket for the following day, making quite sure that she did not simply go at once and leave her aunt. During the two days, she had told her aunt everything about the fire and it had all helped to clear away the lingering sadness of her father's death. Aunt Mary had stories to tell of her childhood in England with her brother and she even had snapshots, happy scenes that Nicola had never seen before. There was peace and Nicola did not really want to go, but she had no choice.

She could not face Blake again and show the same courage.

In the afternoon, Janet came. It was unexpected. Nicola walked into the hall and found Janet just being shown into the house by a smiling Dolores who obviously knew and liked her and Nicola found herself freezing, self-defence surfacing even though she, too, liked the woman who had a claim on Blake.

'I suppose this is unforgivable,' Janet said with a wry grimace as she followed Nicola into the room overlooking the sea. 'I never phoned and I haven't even been in to see Mary yet, but I simply must see Blake.'

Nicola just stared, everything inside seeming to stop.

'But he's not here. He's at the cabin—at least I think he's there.'

'Damn!' Janet sat down with a thump and bit her lip anxiously. 'Well, I dare not go to the cabin. That's strictly out of bounds.' She looked up into Nicola's suddenly pale face. 'I expect you think I'm a lunatic, but the fact is, I've had an offer. There's a new film and I've been offered the lead, but I have to see Blake first. I felt there was something in the wind, some new idea he had and, although he didn't say anything I wanted to know what was in it for me.' She suddenly grinned at Nicola. 'Isn't it mercenary? But Blake really is the best and I'd rather work with him, even though he does drive me to the very edge of murder sometimes.'

'You could ring the cabin,' Nicola suggested. With Janet here and speaking about Blake as if he was just an important director she knew well, Nicola didn't know what to think. Her heart was thumping, her hands wanting to tremble.

'There's no phone there. Blake told me that ages ago. When he's working he's like a bear. If anyone so much as sneezes he roars so he just doesn't let anybody near him. That cabin is completely off-limits.' She sat looking thoughtful. 'I'll have to take this part, I think. If Blake has something he'll not say for ages and even then he might not want me.'

Nicola was just staring at her and the fact seemed to dawn on Janet, her own interests fading as she looked at Nicola's pale face.

'Is anything wrong?' she asked and Nicola sat down too, her legs feeling weak.

'I—I thought... I thought you were at the cabin with Blake.' For a long time Janet simply looked at her and then she sighed.

'Not now and not ever. I told you it was off-limits and I meant it.' She made a wry face and inspected her hands before looking up. 'If Blake ever took anyone there it would be a sort of final step—he would have found the one woman he wanted. I somehow thought it would be you.'

'Blake was just—just looking after me,' Nicola said tremulously. 'My father died and I was in a fire and...'

'I've never known him look after anyone before, except Mary,' Janet said quietly. 'He is what he looks: tough, hard, ruthless. I've never seen him get into a state about anything before either. I saw his face when he brought you down from that church and I saw his face when Martin Cole was leading you on. Blake just doesn't react like that.'

'It was for Aunt Mary, I expect,' Nicola murmured, her mind not really on the conversation. She was thinking about Blake, about his reaction now. He would never forgive her if she had been wrong.

'No,' Janet said softly. 'The moment I saw you, I knew. I've always known that one day somebody would reach Blake, somebody would be able to make him into a normal human being who felt emotion like everyone else. I could never manage it.'

Nicola looked up quickly and Janet smiled, a rather sad look on her face.

'Blake and I were once more than friends,' she confessed. 'It didn't last long and it was a very long time ago. He never really needed me. He's like a mountain, high and unattainable. He walks in the circle of his own power and nothing touches him deeply. You do, though.'

'I—I don't think so,' Nicola whispered. 'I was just part of a plan. He's dealt with it now and, in any case...'

'In any case, you turned him down because you were scared,' Janet finished for her. 'I can see why he's at the cabin, then. I wouldn't dare go now if my life depended on it. A tiger licking his wounds is far too dangerous.'

Nicola's mind was swimming. She had no time to work out what it all meant, but one thing was certain, she had been wrong about Janet being with Blake. Maybe she had been wrong about everything?

'I think there's a film,' she said as Janet stood with a resigned sigh. 'On the plane he was reading a book. He must have read it about three times as we flew over. He seemed to be absorbed.'

'Oh, if only I could find out!' Janet muttered. 'Dare I wait? I just don't know. Look, Nicola, if he gets in touch, tell him I called and tell him why, will you?'

'If he gets in touch,' Nicola promised. 'I'm going home tomorrow, though.'

'You're making a mistake,' Janet assured her quietly. 'Still, if you don't care...'

'I do,' Nicola said with her heart in her eyes and Janet smiled, turning away.

'I wonder if he knows that?' she mused. 'If he does, he'll just come after you. If he doesn't, he might just stay at that cabin for months.'

'Did—did he do that when you left him?' Nicola asked tremulously and Janet turned back, her lips quirking in the wry way Nicola had seen so often on films with this beautiful woman.

'I didn't leave him, Nicola. Blake just stopped noticing me. I was, after all, nothing more than a friend when it all flattened out. He never lost his cool over me, never went white to the lips, never looked as if he would commit murder. Do you have the nerve to go up to the cabin, I wonder?' She looked at Nicola quizzically and then went to see Mary, and Nicola was left feeling utterly lost. Blake had spoken of the sky falling. At that moment it seemed to have fallen on her.

She knew she would not have the nerve to go to the cabin, even if she had known where it was. She was too afraid. If Blake had just wanted her, if it was just desire, then one day he would stop noticing her, too, and she would be left like Janet, hoping, watching for somebody else who would take Blake's life into their hands. She didn't have the courage and, in any case, as Janet had said, she had turned him down.

He had offered, almost demanded to go back to England with her. It would mean that he would have been leaving his work behind for as long as it took. Did that denote any kind of love, any kind of commitment? She just didn't know.

She was having dinner that evening with Mary when the phone rang and Dolores came in to tell Nicola that the call was for her. It would be from Dr Gregory, she knew. He had rung since Blake had left for the cabin, his voice excited about the turn in events that had vindicated his friend. Now he would be wanting to gossip and a call to America would not put him off. It was comforting to think that he would meet her when she arrived back home.

'Hello?' She smiled as she spoke, her mind winging across the seas to Dr Gregory's study, a place she had been in many times and, when Blake's voice came on the line, she was stunned.

'Nicola?' She just stood like a stone, holding the phone tightly, unable to answer and Blake's voice was harsh when he repeated her name. 'Nicola! Answer me for

God's sake! I know you don't want to hear from me and I know you're ready to leave, but just answer!'

'I—I was going to answer. I thought it was Dr Gregory. You—you took me by surprise and...'

'I thought you might have left already,' he said sombrely. 'I suddenly had this feeling that I'd got the dates mixed and it might have been yesterday. It seems to be so long ago...'

Nicola was shocked, almost unable to speak at all. The impression she was getting was just not Blake. The dynamic way he had of speaking was all gone.

'Janet came,' she said hurriedly, not knowing what else to say. 'She wanted to know if you would have a part for her soon because she's had this offer, you see, and she...'

'I don't want to know!' Blake grated. 'What are you talking about Janet for?'

'Well, she asked me and I knew you were working on something.'

'Working?' Blake said bitterly. 'You think I'm working? Do you know what I'm doing here? I'm walking about, round and round, up and down. I must have covered a hundred miles since I left you. I've walked round the cabin, along the beach, round the woods. At night I come back and start again, all round the cabin. God, I'm tired!'

'Blake!' She had never heard him sound like this before, so weary, so lost and she wanted to be able to hold him, comfort him. 'Is—is the book no good then?' she asked shakily. 'I knew you were interested in it, but...'

'Damn the book!' Blake said savagely. Then his voice dropped low. 'Come to me, Nicky!' he begged desperately. 'Please, come to me.'

She was too choked up inside to answer and, before she could, she heard Blake sigh like a condemned man who was to have no reprieve. He just put the phone down and she stared at it in horror. He needed her and she had let him think she would not go. She couldn't ring him back because there was no phone there. He must have driven somewhere to phone her. He must care after all.

Nicola ran back to the dining-room and just burst in on her aunt.

'I've got to get to Blake!' she announced agitatedly. 'I've got to!'

'What is it, Nicola?' Mary went pale and Nicola suddenly saw how stupid it was to let her aunt think something was wrong.

'Oh, it's nothing,' she whispered, sitting down and taking Mary's hand. 'Blake's all right, but he wants me to go to the cabin. He needs me and he thought I wouldn't go so he put the phone down. I can't ring him back. I've got to get there!'

'What about England tomorrow?' Mary asked softly and Nicola looked up with startled eyes. She had forgotten all about England.

'Blake *needs* me!' she insisted almost angrily, and her aunt's face softened.

'You love him, don't you?' she asked with a smile at her niece.

'Oh, yes!' Nicola could not even begin to think of hiding it and Mary nodded with every sign of satisfaction.

'I thought as much. I could feel something in the air between you two. I know Blake. Fetching you here and having you around would normally have driven him straight away from the place, as far away as he could get. That's what I expected. Instead, he hung around and when he couldn't do that any longer he invented a job for you.'

'Do you think he cares?' Nicola asked with a wistful look and her aunt's eyebrows rose sceptically.

'What are they raising in England nowadays, girl, lunatics? Of course he cares. Blake doesn't *need* people, they need him!' She smiled and patted Nicola's hand. 'Pablo knows where the cabin is. He'll drive you up there.'

Pablo seemed to be going painfully slowly and Nicola kept looking at him in agitation. She had just run out of the house with her bag in her hand and nothing else, some dread in her that Blake would have gone away before she got there—they couldn't go fast enough for her.

'I get you there, *señorita*,' Pablo assured her smugly. 'Many times before, I drive this car. I go shopping for the *señora*. I take her for drives. Sometimes I come to the cabin with things for Señor Anderson. I can find the way.'

'Could you find it a little faster?' Nicola asked urgently. 'He might have left already.'

'If so, is no point in hurrying,' Pablo said with devastating logic, and she had to sit back and bite at her nails in silence. After all, she didn't really know how Blake felt. Janet and her aunt had been sure that he cared, but he had never said it. He had asked her to go, though, he had begged and she had never even imagined that Blake could beg.

They turned down to the sea where the road was narrow and lonely and, after what seemed to be a long time, Nicola saw lights through the trees and Pablo grunted in satisfaction, his opinion proved.

'Lights,' he said firmly. 'Señor Anderson is there. I wait for you now?'

She didn't know. Perhaps Blake had simply gone out and left the lights on. It was a long way from anywhere here. She would be stranded if Blake had left. It was some kind of test to give herself, though, and she stopped the car at the end of the short, narrow lane that led to the cabin.

'You can go back, Pablo,' she said determinedly. 'I'm all right.'

He didn't argue and she supposed that, like everyone else, he feared Blake's wrath if he showed his face in this secret and private place. It took only a few minutes to walk to the cabin, but when Pablo had pulled away there was just the sound of the wind in the trees, the quiet wash of the ocean below the cliffs and silence. It was dark by now, but Nicola was not afraid, her eyes were on the place where Blake would be and they never left it.

The place was much grander than she had expected. It was wooden, but not by any stretch of the imagination could it be called a cabin, not any cabin that she could have envisaged. It was like a hunting lodge, some place where a rich man could come for privacy, perhaps for fishing. As she came to the open door and looked into the lighted main room, she could see that it was comfortable too, shining wooden floors with bright rugs and a fireplace built from stone, but Blake was not there.

She saw him then and she felt a burst of shock at the sight of him. He looked almost haggard, his face pale beneath the tan. He was walking into the room from the back and, as he saw her, he just stopped, staring at her as if she was some sort of apparition.

'Nicola?' He just whispered her name, not moving at all even when she stepped into the light of the room. 'You came?' he asked with a sort of bewildered astonishment and she stood quite still because her legs were trembling too much to step forward again.

'I—I thought you . . . You sounded as if you—needed me,' she managed quietly, but Blake never moved.

'I do need you,' he said in a shaken voice. 'But what about you? What do you need?'

There was something about him that tore at her heart, a lonely, empty look and tears tore at her her too, coming without warning.

'I need you too, Blake,' she choked. 'Please don't make me go.'

Blake sprang forward, just dropping the books he had been carrying, letting them fall to the floor as he covered the distance between them and crushed her in his arms.

'When have I ever made you go?' he asked huskily. 'Since the moment I saw you I've tried to keep you near me. I've never wanted you out of my sight.' His hands cupped her face as he lifted it. 'Why did you want to leave me, Nicky?' he asked desperately. 'Why did you tell me you didn't feel anything any more?'

'I—I thought there was Janet. I thought she was coming here with you.'

'Oh, sweetheart!' He rocked her in his arms, his hand stroking her hair. 'Janet was a long time ago and, even then...'

'I know. She told me today.'

Nicola's voice was still filled with tears and Blake drew back far enough to look at her.

'Is that why you came?' he asked quietly, but she shook her head.

'No. I was still going back because I thought you would never forgive me. I came because you phoned and I thought—I hoped...'

'I've needed you from the moment I saw you,' Blake told her gently. 'I needed you even before you opened your green eyes and looked at me from that hospital bed. I love you.'

'Oh, Blake. Why didn't you tell me?' she whispered. 'I might have just gone back and never seen you again.'

'I felt I didn't have the right to tell you. I made you come with me; bullied you into coming to a place you had no wish to see. I couldn't let you go, but I had no rights. I had to have you with me. I loved you, but...'

'It didn't make you nice to me,' Nicola reminded him, looking up into his dark eyes.

'Didn't it, baby?' he asked tenderly. 'I did everything I could for you. I watched over you like a tiger.' His hand ran slowly down her body, brushing her breast, and he smiled seductively. 'I even dressed you.'

Nicola just went on looking up at him with wistful eyes and his hands tightened on her convulsively, his face darkening.

'When you look at me like that I can't think of anything but kissing you,' he said unevenly. 'If I do, you know what will happen. I won't be able to stop. I want you. It's like being so hungry that nothing else enters my mind.'

'I sent Pablo away,' she whispered, looking at him with enormous eyes, feeling herself being drawn into the darkness of Blake's gaze. 'I—I just wanted to be here with you, alone. I haven't anything to sleep in even if you've got another bedroom, and...'

'Don't!' Blake said huskily. 'You're driving me mad. You've been looking at me like that since I first saw you. How long do you think I can resist the invitation?'

'A second?' Nicola asked, silenced when his lips crushed hers and he pulled her closer, his body demanding and powerful against her own. The flames started at once, no pause for the fires to build and Blake kissed her hungrily, his hand holding her face up to his as he drained her lips of all the sweet eagerness.

'Nicky, darling,' he murmured thickly, when his lips left hers and he buried his face in her hair. 'I want to know what this means to you. I have to know because you're not just any woman, not just somebody I want. I'll never want anyone again. I've loved you since I first saw you. If you left me, if you went back, I could only follow you. What else would I do? Where else could I go? Put me out of my misery, sweetheart.'

It was Nicola's turn to comfort and her hands cupped Blake's face as she drew back to look at him with all her feelings in her eyes.

'I love you too, Blake,' she said softly. 'I thought I was afraid of you, but I suppose I was afraid of myself, afraid of all the feelings running through me, feelings I had never had before. I love you so much.'

Blake's eyes were brilliant as he looked down at her and then she was swept into his arms, kisses rained on her face.

'I haven't got two bedrooms,' he said thickly, 'and you don't need anything to sleep in. Come with me, angel. Let me show you how much I need you, how much I'll always need you.'

When the door to the outside world was locked and Nicola lay in Blake's arms, her golden hair spread out over his pillow, he smiled down at her, his restraint easing away any last-minute fears.

'Nothing is going to hurt you again,' he promised gently, trailing kisses over her silken shoulders. 'Tonight you'll sleep with me here and tomorrow I'll take you back.'

'Oh no!' Nicola cried, clutching at him. 'I can't leave you again.'

'Do you think I can leave you?' Blake asked, his eyes beginning to burn down at her. 'I need you here, like this.' He moved over her, his lean, powerful body covering hers possessively. 'I want to marry you, as soon as possible, but I can't sleep without you ever again. We can collect your things and stay here, or we can go back to Mary, or we can go to England—but wherever we go, we're together.'

'Then I don't care where we go,' Nicola sighed, and Blake's lips covered her own until the flames shot up into a dark sky, until their bodies moved together as one, straining to be even closer.

'Look at me, Nicky, darling,' Blake gasped hungrily. 'Look at me again.'

Nicola opened her eyes, dazed with love, not knowing what he wanted to see, but his burning gaze held hers and his colour darkened with passion, his lips closing over her cry as he entered her swiftly and strongly. Her body closed round him silkily and Blake took them both through a velvet universe that was filled with golden stars.

When they finally came back to earth and Nicola opened her eyes, Blake was watching her, his face filled with adoration.

'You're everything your eyes promised me,' he said unevenly. 'At first, I couldn't believe the way you looked at me. I've had plenty of looks thrown my way at times, women who were trying to edge their way into a part in some film, women who imagined it would be nice to be attached to a film director.'

'Like Dorette Ingham,' Nicola said with smile.

'Like Dorette,' he agreed, laughing down at her. 'But you looked at me and rocked my world. Your eyes dazzled me, pleaded with me, made me promises that stopped my breath.'

'It was disgraceful,' Nicola murmured, her cheeks flushing hotly.

'Shameful.' His lips gently lingered at the corner of her mouth. 'And when I touched you it was unbelievable, as if you were already part of me.'

'I wanted to be,' Nicola whispered, and his face darkened to passion again as he gathered her closer.

'Now you are,' he reminded her huskily. 'We just go up in flames, don't we?' His lips trailed heated kisses over her face, his mouth seeking hers again and again. 'Why didn't you bring more clothes, you little scatterbrain?' he groaned. 'Surely you knew I wouldn't let you go again? I'll have to take you back for more things and we'll get involved with people.'

'You're grumbling,' Nicola laughed against his lips and his hands tightened convulsively.

'I don't want to share you,' he growled, back to being the old Blake who made her tremble. 'I don't want to see anyone else for a long time.'

'We could drive back in the morning and collect my things,' Nicola suggested softly. 'Then, as far as anyone is concerned, we would be working here. Nobody has the nerve to come to the cabin when you're working.'

'Sneaky,' Blake said admiringly, grinning down at her like a satisfied tiger. 'Practical too. It's a good place to hide out until we're married.'

'Except that Aunt Mary would feel left out and lonely,' Nicola pointed out, winding her arms around his neck.

'Not Mary,' he said emphatically. 'Mary has a hectic social life in spite of her disability. Pablo drives her all over the place. She's been just sitting around with you here, but it was only to be with you until you recovered. Mary will be off like a shot the moment we're away.'

'But she wanted me there!' Nicola protested. 'She needed me.'

'She wanted you to come because you're her niece, the daughter of her very much loved brother,' Blake said huskily. 'But I was the one who needed you. When I had to go to the location, I was frantic. I couldn't settle without you.'

'So you invented a job for me,' Nicola pronounced, remembering her aunt's words. 'You could have managed with just about anybody writing down your orders.'

'It was more civilised than dragging you off by the hair,' Blake murmured. 'I didn't want just anybody close to me. I wanted you.'

'But was I useful?' Nicola insisted, looking up at him severely. 'Was I any good?'

A seductive smile tilted his mouth and his dark gaze flashed over her face and rested on her soft lips.

'Honey, you were terrific,' he said huskily.

MILLS & BOON

Christmas Treasures

Unwrap the romance this Christmas

Four exciting new Romances by favourite Mills & Boon
authors especially for you this Christmas.

A Christmas Wish - Betty Neels
Always Christmas - Eva Rutland
Reform Of The Rake - Catherine George
Christmas Masquerade - Debbie Macomber

Published: November 1994

Available from WH Smith, John Menzies,
Volume One, Forbuoys, Martins, Woolworths,
Tesco, Asda, Safeway and other paperback
stockists.

SPECIAL PRICE : £5.70
(4 BOOKS FOR THE PRICE OF 3)

THREE LOVE STORIES...

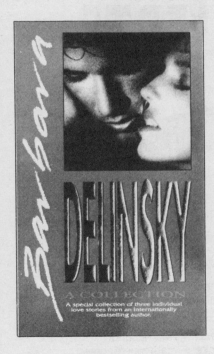

A beautiful collection of three individual love stories from *New York Times* bestselling author Barbara Delinsky – each featuring the charming and irrepressible matchmaker, Victoria Lesser.

A very collectable volume, offering new fans the chance to sample some of Delinsky's earlier works and for long-time fans to collect an edition to treasure.

W⊕RLDWIDE

AVAILABLE FROM SEPTEMBER   **PRICED £4.99**

Available from WH Smith, John Menzies, Volume One, Forbuoys, Martins, Woolworths, Tesco, Asda, Safeway and other paperback stockists.

NORA ROBERTS

A COLLECTION

From the best-selling author of *Hot Ice* and *Sweet Revenge*
comes a dazzling collection of three early novels,
beautifully presented in one absorbing volume.

THE LAST HONEST WOMAN
DANCE TO THE PIPER
SKIN DEEP

Three impulsive sisters, three intimate encounters, three
sensuous and unforgettable love stories.

AVAILABLE NOW   **PRICE £4.99**

WORLDWIDE

*Available from WH Smith, John Menzies, Volume One, Forbuoys, Martins,
Woolworths, Tesco, Asda, Safeway and other paperback stockists.*

Cruel Legacy

PENNY JORDAN

Cruel Legacy

When tragedy strikes, the wounds are deep and irrevocable

One man's untimely death deprives a wife of her husband, robs a man of his job and offers someone else the chance of a lifetime...

Suicide — the only way out for Andrew Ryecart, facing crippling debt. An end to his troubles, but for those he leaves behind the problems are just beginning, as the repercussions of this most desperate of acts reach out and touch the lives of six different people — changing them forever.

Special large-format paperback edition

OCTOBER
£8.99

W❂RLDWIDE

Available from WH Smith, John Menzies, Volume One, Forbuoys, Martins, Woolworths, Tesco, Asda, Safeway and other paperback stockists.

NORA ROBERTS

◆

HOT ICE

Reckless and beautiful, Whitney MacAllister had the cash and the connections.

Street-wise and good-looking, Douglas Lord had the stolen documents leading to a fabulous hidden fortune.

It was a business proposition — pure and simple. But the race to find the treasure, from Manhattan to Madagascar, was only part of the game.

Don't miss Nora Roberts' sizzling novel of red hot passion and cold hard cash.

AVAILABLE NOW   **PRICE £4.99**

W⬤RLDWIDE

Available from WH Smith, John Menzies, Volume One, Forbuoys, Martins, Woolworths, Tesco, Asda, Safeway and other paperback stockists.

Next Month's Romances

Each month you can choose from a wide variety of romance with Mills & Boon. Below are the new titles to look out for next month, why not ask either Mills & Boon Reader Service or your Newsagent to reserve you a copy of the titles you want to buy – just tick the titles you would like and either post to Reader Service or take it to any Newsagent and ask them to order your books.

Please save me the following titles: Please tick ✓

Title	Author	
A VERY STYLISH AFFAIR	Emma Darcy	
ELEMENT OF RISK	Robyn Donald	
TO HAVE AND TO HOLD	Sally Wentworth	
BURDEN OF INNOCENCE	Patricia Wilson	
LOVERS NOT FRIENDS	Helen Brooks	
THREADS OF DESTINY	Sara Wood	
INNOCENT DECEIVER	Lilian Peake	
WHISPER OF SCANDAL	Kathryn Ross	
CALYPSO'S ENCHANTMENT	Kate Walker	
SAVING THE DEVIL	Sophie Weston	
BETWEEN TWO LOVES	Rosemary Hammond	
DREAM MAN	Quinn Wilder	
STEP IN THE DARK	Marjorie Lewty	
LOVESTORM	Jennifer Taylor	
DECEPTIVE DESIRE	Sally Carr	
A PASSIONATE DECEIT	Kate Proctor	

If you would like to order these books in addition to your regular subscription from Mills & Boon Reader Service please send £1.90 per title to: Mills & Boon Reader Service, Freepost, P.O. Box 236, Croydon, Surrey, CR9 9EL, quote your Subscriber No:................................... (if applicable) and complete the name and address details below. Alternatively, these books are available from many local Newsagents including W H Smith, J Menzies, Martins and other paperback stockists from 9 December 1994.

Name:..

Address:..

....Post Code:........................

To Retailer: If you would like to stock M&B books please contact your regular book/magazine wholesaler for details.

You may be mailed with offers from other reputable companies as a result of this application. If you would rather not take advantage of these opportunities please tick box. ☐